LET BHUTTO EAT GRASS

Shaunak Agarkhedkar

LET BHUTTO
EAT GRASS

Shaunak Agarkhedkar

Twitter.com/ShaunakSA

ISBN-13: 978-1973730354
ISBN-10: 1973730359

Typeset in Adobe Caslon Pro by the author.

For Shikha

"If India builds the bomb, we will eat grass or leaves, even go hungry, but we will get one of our own."
—Zulfikar Ali Bhutto
Minister of Foreign Affairs, Pakistan
11 March 1965

Salute the sappers, all you fighting men;
All you great guns and tanks and lorries, bow!
Bow down, bazooka, bayonet and Bren.
Without the sapper, where would you be now?

The bridge is broken, mines are in the hay.
A thousand deaths are hidden in the grass.
But here's the sapper—he will find a way:
And, you great guns, salute them as they pass.

—A. P. Herbert
11 February 1945

PROLOGUE

1971, Moulvi Bazar (East Pakistan)

Drawn with swift, practised ease, the seven-inch stiletto blade emerged from its scabbard with only the softest rasp that blended unheard into the noise of the rain. The soldier stood two yards away, his rifle casually slung across his back. He remained oblivious till the moment a heavy hand reached over his left shoulder and clamped across his mouth. The wet mud that coated it entered his nostrils, clogging them. As his head was jerked back and he lost his footing, the soldier cried out, but the only sound he heard was the sharp exhalation of his assailant. Whatever little training he had received before being rushed east to this post deserted him, and he clawed desperately at the hand that was suffocating him. Time seemed to slow down. He fell back, vaguely aware of a burning sensation at the right side of his neck. Then, a sharp jolt of pain shot inward, searing his throat and sinews. His eyes flew wide open, but all he could see were dark leaves and stars too bright to be real. He was on his back now, his limbs flailing, like a drowning man. The pair of legs that had wrapped around his waist pinned him down. Choking on his own blood, the young soldier's lungs gurgled to clear his airway. By then the stiletto had driven forward remorselessly, severing the carotid artery. As blood

1

supply to his brain collapsed, his dying scream emerged as an awful, sibilant hiss from the severed windpipe.

Captain Sablok wiped the blade clean on his victim's khaki shirt and pushed the corpse away. Rising to his feet, he sheathed his trusty stiletto with a satisfying click. He had spent the last four hours lying prone in the dark rice fields and watching the bridge, waiting for the right moment. It had taken forever, but at long last, the majority of the platoon had crossed over to patrol the northern side of the bridge, leaving only two soldiers at his end. Well, at least the wait had been worth it. He looked down at the corpse and spat in distaste. The soldier's bowels had released as he died and the rancid smell of shit mixed with the coppery tang of blood still spurting from the severed carotid. Thankfully, he didn't have to wait long. Havildar Singh emerged from the gloom to his left and, catching Sablok's gaze, gave a quick nod: the other soldier had been dispatched. Sablok watched as Singh then bent down and, grabbing a handful of hair to extend the neck, severed the dead man's head with an indifferent slash of a machete-like blade to which the Mukti Bahini had introduced him. Sablok smiled. This action at the bridge had not been part of the original plan, but when he had proposed it, Singh hadn't hesitated even for a second. They arranged the bodies such that they appeared to be resting against the trunk of the tree with their heads on their laps—Sablok's grim joke. Then, the two men melted into the dark landscape to the east.

Sablok and Singh were sappers with the Indian Army. They had volunteered, separately, after the extent of Pakistan's genocidal campaign against its own Bengali populace became apparent. The first time they had met each other was at a ramshackle camp north of Agartala three months earlier, in May. Since then the two had infiltrated deep into East Pakistan half a dozen times. The first four missions had been aggressive; they had led a team of Mukti Bahini that had ambushed patrols and killed Pakistani soldiers. The last two missions had seen Sablok and Singh slip in quietly without any support to reconnoitre terrain. The current one, too, had begun as a reconnaissance mission. They had been charged with the responsibility of mapping the lay of the land, based on which the axis of advance would be chosen for the eventual Indian assault. Everything had been going as planned until the platoon of soldiers at the bridge they had been observing from

2

afar caught a family fleeing towards India. The mother's screams soon rent the air. Sablok and Singh couldn't intervene: they were too far away and, equipped only with their rifles and side arms, there was no way they could have taken on an entire platoon. All they could do was grit their teeth as each soldier crested the elevated road, went down the other side out of their sight, and had his way with the woman. Sablok was no stranger to violence, having served with distinction on the western front in '65. Even so, the gruesome accounts of brutality related by Bengali refugees who had crossed the border to camps in India had seemed to have a surreal, fictional quality that had kept them at a comfortable distance from everyday reality. Now, though, there was no avoiding what was happening in front of his eyes. A loud hoot grabbed his attention: a soldier put his muddy boot on the neck of the woman's husband and began to slowly squeeze life out of his battered body. Cheered on by his mates, the soldier would squeeze till the man was almost gone, then let go for a while before squeezing again. It reminded Sablok of a kitten tormenting a mouse and bile rose in his throat. Further down the road, a pair of soldiers had cornered a child of five or six years. The boy's shriek was abruptly cut off when his distended belly was pierced through by a bayonet. The mother couldn't have seen it from where she lay, but her agonised scream indicated that she knew. By then the father was dead of asphyxiation. The mother survived for another hour. That's when he had decided. The men were in uniform—the dull khaki of the Pakistan Army—but there was no honour in what they had done. The hapless family deserved revenge. Some blood would have to be spilt. Singh agreed.

'These aren't soldiers, sir,' he spat out. 'They're scum.'

The impromptu mission had cost them precious time, though, and Sablok was keeping a close watch on the chronometer on his left wrist. Staying within two hundred yards of the Kushiyara River and wading through knee-high mud in rice fields, it had taken them nearly an hour to reach the Manu, a tributary of the Kushiyara that flowed from the south and impeded their way. A rowboat stood on the near bank, ten yards above the swollen river's edge, exactly where they had been promised it would be. Battling against a rampaging current that sought to wash them away to the larger Kushiyara, they took considerably longer than expected to cross over and pull the boat up the other side.

Both men were exhausted, but there was no time to rest. Two large swamps and certain death lay directly east of their position, so they headed south instead. Five miles from the large Pakistani garrison at Moulvi Bazar, they turned south-east, keeping as close to the edge of the Farahanga Beel as they dared, to avoid Pakistani patrols. They skirted Mathiura lake at 3:30 a.m. and found themselves, at long last, on solid ground.

Sablok retrieved a map from his pocket and consulted it, taking care to remain flat in a depression in the ground. Their intended destination, the Kadamtala border, was nineteen miles away, a distance they were unlikely to cover in three hours. Rangauti was the nearest Indian border, just twelve miles from their location. But it was right next to two East Pakistani towns and would certainly be well-patrolled. The third option, of course, was to go to ground till dusk. He looked askance at Singh. In the summer of '63, the importance of consulting Havildars had been relentlessly hammered into him and his mates at Doon until it was internalised. Havildar Singh was six years older than Sablok. More important, while Sablok's professional life began at twenty-one as a Second Lieutenant, Singh had become a soldier at seventeen and had served nearly twenty years in uniform, the last ten devoted to keeping callow Second Lieutenants from getting themselves and their platoons killed.

'Rangauti,' Singh replied without hesitation, echoing Sablok's own exhaustion.

Bisecting the road between the towns of Bizli and Shamshernagar, they reached a point two miles from the border. It was just after 5:30 a.m. and the eastern horizon was lightening under a dark layer of clouds. They ran fast, each man scanning his own arcs for any signs of a patrol or border post. The terrain was flat and offered no cover. It was only a matter of time before they would be spotted. To the left, they saw the Manu river once again, slightly emaciated, thirty miles closer to its source. In the distance, they could make out the silhouettes of houses in Rangauti, almost within reach. Sablok's lungs burned with the intensity of an overworked mortar tube. Singh was fifteen yards ahead of him, but beginning to tire.

Sablok caught up with him: 'I've seen Generals run faster, old man.'

In response, the Havildar dug deep within himself and somehow found the strength to speed up. Moments later they heard the tell-tale high-pitched whistle of a mortar somewhere to the right. They dived to hug the earth. Fifty yards to the left, the ground exploded, deafening them momentarily. Within seconds, they were up and running again, brushing off debris and veering to the south-east to put more distance between themselves and the point where the mortar had landed. Another loud whistle and, once again, they dropped to the ground. This one landed further away, about seventy yards to the north.

About five hundred yards ahead, they could see the meandering Manu which served as the border near Rangauti. Sablok threw off his rucksack. Every pound counted.

Four hundred yards.

A few huts came up on their right, concealing them from the mortar crew.

'Drop the sack!' he shouted to Singh.

The older man heard him and cast it off. They were both going flat out now, carrying only their weapons, bayonet affixed to each man's rifle and ready for anyone foolish enough to block their path.

Three hundred yards.

They were back in the open and, almost immediately, the screaming whistle returned, passing overhead to land some distance away. Sablok glanced up as he ran; Singh didn't even bother to crouch, preferring to trust his judgement that the mortar crew were second-rate.

Two hundred yards.

Sablok could hear the river now, a gentle gurgle barely louder than his own breathing, the exact sound the young soldier's drowning lungs had made as he lay bleeding from Sablok's stiletto. Its bank was fifty yards ahead and, as the next inevitable whistle sounded, Singh reached its edge. The explosions were nearly simultaneous and the blast wave knocked both men down. Sablok was dazed; his ears rang loudly. There was blood streaming from his nose and right ear. He struggled to orient himself within the thick cloud of mud. Rushing forward, his body feeling no pain at all, he stumbled over Singh. The Havildar's eyes were open and stared, his right leg had been blown clean off just below the knee, and Sablok could see a jagged white edge of the tibia poking through red flesh. Singh blinked, then scrambled to try and get to his feet. Faced with overwhelming shock, Sablok's mind had shut down all thought and fallen back on the primitive, more dependable terrain of instinct. He hoisted Singh onto his shoulders and stepped into the current, his heart pounding deafeningly. The water was freezing and fast and, across it, he could see a patrol. Its soldiers took position to face him, but their uniforms and insignias remained unclear. Downstream the Manu flowed back into East Pakistan and headed straight for Sharifpur. Wading upstream was impossible, not with Singh weighing him down. Hoping the patrol that faced him was an Indian one, he pushed on, fighting the raging river. A mortar screamed past but landed a safe distance away. In response, another flew up from somewhere in front of him and headed towards Sharifpur, a warning that was promptly heeded. Four men rushed down the left bank and reached for him. He pushed the first one back in anger, then got a good look at his uniform; it wasn't the dull khaki of the Pakistanis and the insignia sported the Sarnath Lions. The soldier was screaming at him. His words didn't penetrate the fog of Sablok's consciousness, but the Lions did. He handed Singh over to the care of two soldiers and leaned on a third for support. He made it across the river but collapsed before the steep slope of the far bank.

A blur of field hospitals followed. They cut into Sablok's left leg thrice, removing shrapnel from the anti-personnel mine that Singh had unwittingly triggered. The last of seven fragments was, the surgeon decided, too close to the femoral artery to operate; Captain Sablok would just have to learn to live with that souvenir from East Pakistan. A few days later, when Sablok emerged from the fog of general anaesthesia and grogginess, it was raining heavily. That night he experienced his first nightmare since early childhood, one of many to come about the bayoneted child and its parents.

The next morning, he had a visitor; word had reached his handlers that he was out of surgery and conscious. The visitor was a new face but that didn't bother Sablok: all spooks looked more or less the same anyway. The debrief proceeded well until they got to the point where the soldiers had discovered the Bengali family hiding in a grove about fifty yards from the road, waiting for dusk. After that, the next detail Sablok said he remembered was the first mortar whistling in; everything in between was blank. After half an hour of persistent probing, the spook sighed in disappointment. His callous expression rankled Sablok.

'Why don't you ask Havildar Singh?' Sablok grunted through the pain.

'Singh died a few minutes after you were rescued. The mine severed an artery. Without a tourniquet...'

The words that followed did not register. Sablok could still see the spook's lips move, but his mind seemed incapable of moving beyond the fact of Singh's death.

The spook reached over after a few moments and shook Sablok's shoulder, bringing him back to the conversation.

'Captain, we need to know what happened. Did you perform any reconnaissance at all on the mission? We could not find any maps on either you or Singh. Do you remember anything at all?'

Sablok had suddenly tired of the whole affair and wanted nothing more to do with it.

'I can't remember what happened,' he said, speaking slowly and enunciating each word. 'But I might remember key features about the terrain.'

For the first time since his arrival at Sablok's ward, the spook's expression changed, relief apparent on his face. He retrieved a series of maps from the briefcase along with a pencil and held them out for Sablok, but the injured man made no attempt to take them from him.

'Havildar Singh's son is in high school, I think. Singh had hoped that he would grow up to be an officer in his own regiment,' Sablok said, his eyes locked on the spook's. 'Since Singh died doing what you asked him to...'

The spook sighed. It seemed exaggerated to Sablok, but he said nothing.

'We don't react well to blackmail, Captain.'

Sablok nodded and managed a half-smile, half-grimace. Moments passed with each man trying to stare the other down. Finally, the spook returned the maps and the pencil to the briefcase and left. He returned the next day carrying a letter for Sablok.

'Havildar Singh's son will be cared for,' he said.

Sablok read the letter and smiled despite the pain in his leg.

'Do you still have those maps? I'll need the pencil too,' he said.

That evening Sablok asked the doctor for a prognosis. The sharp pain that intruded into his consciousness, despite what the nurse had assured him was the recommended dose of morphine, carried within it the possibility of terrible news of his own.

'We've had to cut away parts of your muscle tissue, Captain. Besides, the fragment that remains is worryingly close to an artery. I'd recommend a desk job from here on.'

The surgeon was a Lieutenant Colonel in the Medical Corps, and it did not behove a mere Captain to dispute his assessment.

'What if you take the leg off and fit me with a prosthetic, sir? Soldiers have served with artificial limbs.'

The surgeon's eyes narrowed. 'You want me to take your leg off?'

'Havildar Singh lost his life, sir. A limb seems trivial against that.'

The surgeon made it clear, without uttering a syllable that, were it not for the trauma suffered, he would consider the young man an idiot. Then he mustered what little patience remained after two weeks of performing surgery after surgery on the mangled meat that returned from East Pakistan.

'An amputation would require the removal of your knee, Captain,' he said, stressing the rank for effect. 'Believe me, your natural knee is a hundred times more comfortable than a prosthetic. In any event, Captain, you will not run five k.m. in twenty-eight minutes ever again.'

Sablok was nothing if not obstinate. 'If it's only a question of comfort, sir, I'm willing to try it.'

The surgeon's patience ran out.

'It is my professional assessment that you do not need an amputation, and that is what your file will say, young man. I suggest you reconcile yourself to life with all limbs more or less intact. Now if you'll excuse me, there are other patients in need of my attention,' he said, sternly, before moving on.

In December '71, as General Sagat Singh's men were racing across the Meghna less than seventy miles from Rangauti, avenging Captain Sablok's career, Havildar Singh's life, and the lives of hundreds of thousands of Bengalis, Sablok was sent to Military Hospital Kirkee on the outskirts of Pune. The surgeries he'd undergone had damaged the musculature of his leg. Sablok had to learn how to walk again, and that took ages. But despite three months of physical therapy and very little sleep, the best he could do by March '72 was run a few yards before collapsing in pain. He could walk long distances, though, and that would have to do.

Throughout convalescence, he had received only one other visitor, his mother. Her first visit was a tearful hour spent cursing the stars and thanking the gods, with the last fifteen minutes devoted to making excuses for his father's absence. The second and last one was shorter and quieter, but the excuses had remained the same.

The day before his departure from M.H. Kirkee, the nurse informed him that there was a phone call for him from a Mr Jagjit Arora.

'General Jagjit Singh Arora?' Sablok asked wide-eyed, referring to the General Officer Commanding-in-Chief of the Eastern Command.

The nurse chuckled.

'No, Captain. I asked him twice. It's a Mr Jagjit Arora from New Delhi.'

Sablok had no desire to speak to any Mr Arora.

'Tell him I'm asleep,' he said.

Ten minutes later, the adjutant of the hospital marched in.

'On your feet, Captain. There's a phone call for you. And I won't have any more of this nonsense about telling them you're asleep when you're clearly wide awake.'

There was nothing for it but to accompany the adjutant to his cabin and take the call.

'So, you are up and about now, I hope, young man?' The voice on the other end said in introduction. 'In case you're wondering who I am, you served with my son in '65.'

In '65, Sablok had served with a Captain Arora who, unfortunately, had succumbed to a large calibre bullet near the outskirts of Lahore. So this Jagjit Arora was his father who, for some reason, had sufficient pull to get a Lieutenant Colonel to act as a messenger.

'So, how are you planning to spend the rest of your life, Captain? Looking after the logistics of visiting colonels and generals at some command or the other, checking to make sure the bedding is clean at the guest house and the toilets have been scrubbed?'

Sablok gritted his teeth. If this was meant to be a courtesy call, Arora wasn't doing a very good job. After a pause, he managed a reply.

'Officers have made it to command despite more grievous injuries, sir,' he said, his voice tight.

'Some have, I'll give you that, Captain. But I don't think any of them had been diagnosed with Gross Stress Reaction.'

Sablok felt light-headed. He reached for the table to steady himself.

'It's in your file, Captain: nightmares, difficulty in falling asleep, loss of memory. Whatever you saw or suffered in Sylhet must have been horrific. The diagnosis has been in your file for months now. They won't put you in command, not even if your father throws his considerable weight—'

'How the hell would you…' Sablok bit back his angry retort. Arora's reference to his father was unwelcome. He took a deep breath. 'Never mind, sir. I suppose it's just as well, considering I got Havildar Singh killed.'

Arora fell silent for a while. Sablok was about to tap the telephone cradle to check if they had been disconnected when Arora spoke. 'Why don't you come work for us? I can't promise much, but at least you won't be stuck nannying some general and his family while they visit.'

'And what is it that you do, sir?' Sablok asked, unable to keep from sounding sardonic.

'Oh! You already know that, Captain. We were the ones that sent you into Bangladesh in the first place.'

CHAPTER ONE

1974, New Delhi (India)

Each corner of the dimly lit stairwell sported a dull red fresco. Some of the modern-day Michaelangelos that curated them had also provided the miasma of ammonia for a touch of the avant-garde. The dust-caked stairs, the walls grimy with body oils—everything about the place suggested grave neglect. Only the absence of visitors and louts kept this government office from being confused for the municipal building down the street. If a casual visitor somehow made it past the rusty barbed wire fence and two old men on sentry duty outside the compound, the robust wrought iron gate on the first-floor landing and the four disinterested-looking factotums standing guard behind it would turn the visitor back. This office was not open to the public.

Footsteps from the stairs below earned an indifferent glance from the four, casual enough to suggest that the rooms guarded by them lacked value. They were present, it appeared, merely as a tick-mark on some bureaucratic checklist. The well-maintained gate was incongruous with that sentiment, but casual visitors to government buildings in India expected the absurd, so it did not matter much. A familiar, middle-aged man dressed in a plain white shirt and mahogany brown trousers, his shoes freshly shined, hair shorn close to the scalp, rounded the corner of the landing between the ground and first floors. He held out his ID. The man in charge nodded once; his minion unlocked the gate. The others stood a bit straighter, more alert, and responded lustily to the man's simple 'Jai Hind'. He used to be a soldier, they knew, and that made him a kindred.

The organisation Sablok worked for was young. It had been birthed by an unwilling mother. Undernourished and denied resources, initially, it had subsisted on with scraps thrown out by other, fatter departments. When fortunes changed in '71, resources no longer had to be begged for; the sudden influx of analysts and Case Officers meant that some had to work from dilapidated buildings that even the municipal authorities—acknowledged experts in decrepitude—did not fancy. Commandeered temporarily till the proposed offices came up at a large plot of land allotted to the organisation, the building housed those exiled from the main host because they lacked sufficient pull. Here they were far from the hallowed corridors patrolled by Section Chiefs and Department Heads, and every opportunity to visit Main on parole to schmooze higher beings, if only for a few hours, was jealously guarded. A few of the hundred-odd people that worked in the dilapidated building, though, were glad to leave behind passive-aggressive departmental politics and the attendant misery. Mostly middle-aged or older, they had grown to appreciate the dark after years spent working in shadows. The young and ambitious pitied them.

Sablok was counted among those who were pitied. His desk stood at the back of a room that he shared with two other analysts in the north wing of the building, shielded by three steel cabinets and one large safe. Neatly piled on his desk were pages holding information from diplomats, Residents, and field agents. At the very top, by virtue of having arrived last, was a low priority cable from the Indian High Commission in Islamabad, dispatched by the Resident almost as an afterthought. Such missives allowed the Resident to continue paying the lovely PIA stewardess and retain her as an asset. Like thousands of other cables that came in each week, this one should have been indexed without much thought and forgotten by lunchtime. Sablok read it carefully, noted the names and abbreviations in it, and sought out more information from other sources. In his experience, pretty women heard and understood a lot more than they were given credit for. People tended to assume that they weren't very smart, and were given to boast in their presence without much regard for consequences.

He ruffled through the bottom shelf of his document cabinet and came away with three large files, his notes compiled over the past two years of service in support of the Pakistan section. They were exhaustive, but he could not find what was needed. They did point him towards a few end documents, though, and he copied the serial numbers of those documents onto a blank page. This aspect of the job was tedious and often fobbed off on the unsuspecting, in favour of tasks that demanded action of some sort. Sablok, however, had suffered enough action for a lifetime and did not mind the measured slog through mountains of typed text. Softly humming Rafi, he read page after page about the who's who of the Pakistani establishment. When he was satisfied that he hadn't missed anyone, he committed the names and serial numbers to memory and burned the list in the metal bin beside his desk. The information he now sought was locked away in files located in the basement of Main. The Archives were meant to represent the collective memory of the Wing, a flourishing anthology of experiences gained through sweat and blood. But in keeping with the extreme paranoia of secret organisations, which was exaggerated in the case of the Wing by a deep-rooted cultural belief in the ephemerality of everything except the soul, the Archives remained a desiccated husk that almost always disappointed those supplicants that prayed at its altar. It was always more productive to tap personal relationships and ask questions, but Sablok had developed none that could help. Main was a mile away. He walked.

The compound had one entrance. To the uninitiated, it was another obscure hive of middling bureaucrats in a city where they swarmed in every crevice. Its distinct lack of the accoutrements of political power meant that it was hardly worth a second glance. The signboards were old and dusty, and the letters on them had long faded into incomprehensibility. Neither of the two men guarding the gate appeared armed. When Sablok showed them his identification, they waved him in, shut the gate behind him, and resumed their private conversation. Walking along the path to the building, he passed the guardhouse to the left. Even though the windows were closed and curtains were drawn, he had the feeling that he was being watched. Inside the building, two more guards carefully compared his particulars

13

with details in a register. Only when they were convinced that he belonged there did they let him descend the stairs. The pretence that those guarding the place couldn't care less had disappeared; this bunch was overtly switched on. Because Sablok was empty handed, the guards manning the entrance to the Archives waved him in.

Winter was still a few weeks away in New Delhi, and he soaked in the warm, muggy weather that the city suffered instead of a proper monsoon. It was just as well; rain brought with it a sense of impending doom. Despite ideal weather conditions, the long walk followed by a climb down three sets of stairs had awoken the piece of shrapnel lodged in his left thigh to a day of possibilities, and he found himself favouring his right leg more than usual as he stepped into the cold, crypt-like confines.

He filled out a form requisitioning specific files by serial number, and another that requested a fishing expedition for any information on three Pakistani nationals. The forms asked for a purpose; 'For corroboration,' he wrote. Ambiguity was definitely a virtue and, although the lady manning the desk frowned when she read those words, she disappeared to get the information requested without complaint. It was a little after 9 a.m., and the place was empty. Sablok stood at the desk waiting, the pain in his leg morphing into a dull ache that he knew from experience would linger for days. The ache brought on his own winter of discontent, reminding him of the time when he could easily endure hours and hours of drill beside Chetwood at IMA. He was struck by the futility of what he was doing and suddenly, all he wanted to do was to head home and nurse the perfectly misty surface of a thick, heavy glass as the whisky inside burned to vanquish the ice before assaulting his agony. He turned to the exit and took two steps towards it before stopping and turning back, his escape interrupted by the sound of footsteps ringing on the linoleum floor.

The woman walked in, carrying a thick stack of documents.

'I think there has been a mistake,' Sablok blurted out in surprise. 'The people I'm looking into aren't prominent enough to merit so many pages.'

She eyed the sweat on his brow with ill-concealed distaste.

'Perhaps if you bothered to read the documents before questioning my competence…'

He was no longer questioning her competence when he finished reading them several hours later.

The Section Chief's office was on the fourth floor of Main. Sablok ignored the ache in his leg and ran up the stairs. Mishra's assistant stopped him from entering and demanded to know his business. Beads of sweat dripping from his brow, he explained that he needed to brief the chief on an emerging situation. She offered him a watered-down smile, asked him to take a seat, and took a note inside. Sablok had barely finished mopping the sweat off his face when Mishra summoned him.

'What emerging situation would you like to brief me about, Captain?' His tone discounted the possibility of an analyst digging up a crisis; the cables were only sent for indexing after they had been evaluated by the Duty Officer and deemed not critical. Sablok ignored the insinuation and briefed him about the PIA cable and his research within the Archives.

'This fellow, Sultan Mahmood—the one leading this team—is one of their best, sir. Double master's from Manchester in control systems and nuclear engineering, years of experience running their first nuclear reactor at Karachi. His peers at Manchester even acknowledged him an expert on the American Manhattan Project.'

'Wasn't that the programme to build a bomb?'

'Yes, sir. Apparently, it is a very complicated process. But this fellow is an expert. And it turns out he was abruptly moved from the nuclear plant to their atomic commission's Research Directorate earlier this year. Now he's leading a team to Amsterdam. It's an unplanned trip, sir; they had to buy first class seats.'

He waited. Life and his instructors had both taught him the importance of holding some firepower in reserve.

The older man sighed. 'We already know they're scrambling to get their hands on a nuclear bomb, Captain; they've been at it for more than a decade now. After burning through precious foreign exchange to send their people overseas for training and research, they've got a big fat egg to show for it. Pakistan cannot build its own bomb because it is a feudal nation state. No number of scientific teams will change that, not in our lifetime.'

Sablok could not dispute the argument. Mishra was rumoured to have spent the better part of a decade in Pakistan as an Illegal in-country until arthritis had forced him to return to India, and even the Secretary—the head of the Wing—was rumoured to defer to Mishra's wisdom when it came to matters involving Pakistan.

'Sir, there's more.'

'There always is with the Pakistanis, Captain. Please hurry up. I have a meeting in five minutes.'

'They're being chaperoned by a diplomat named Moraad Baksh. He served in India for eleven years before being non-grata'd back in '66.'

'So they're recycling diplomats now. Or are you suggesting he's one of Jilani Khan's own?' Mishra asked, referring to the head of the ISI.

'I'm certain he is.'

'Quite possible. But this isn't out of the ordinary. They probably sent him to make sure none of the others defect. The Punjabis of Rawalpindi wouldn't entrust a Balochi with greater responsibility.'

'I think it's worth investigating, sir.'

'With what resources?'

'Well, a team in Pakistan and one in Europe...'

'Two teams? You don't work for the Americans, Captain. Our resources are finite, and I have none to spare at the moment. The ungrateful bastards are plotting to kill Bangabandhu, and my agents are scrambling to stop them.'

'What about Europe?'

Mishra guffawed. 'If you think you can get that miserly old man of the European section to give you agents for a private hobby, you're really deluding yourself, Captain. Perhaps it might help to cut back on the whisky a bit.'

Back in his own office, Sablok tried to go through the remaining documents awaiting his attention. But the uneasy feeling he had about Sultan Mahmood and Moraad Baksh gnawed at him. After a lot of thought, he dialled a number on the Wing's internal telephone network.

'Arora saab, this is Sablok. Have you had lunch yet, sir?'

CHAPTER TWO

Three plates of mutton seekh kebabs were enough to make Sablok feel like a stuffed pakoda himself, but his portly companion happily dug into a fourth one. The spices were turning his prominent nose the colour of saffron, but the only concession he made for them was to take an occasional gulp from a tall glass of sweet lassi.

'Sure you won't have some more, Sablok? This meat is so tender, I could swear the chef's made a Faustian bargain.'

A thin sheen of sweat glazed his jowly face despite the wall-mounted fan's unwavering attention. Eyes half closed, he delighted in chewing each morsel of minced muscle and cartilage, and the occasional onion, in a carnal display that at once intrigued and frightened Sablok. Fifty-three, balding, with pudgy fingers and a nose to be envied, the man's stomach spoke of aloo paranthas for breakfast—with dollops of ghee, of course—and a genetic affection for kukkad and mutton.

'One of these days the remaining goats of this country will hunt you down,' Sablok remarked.

'Not if I eat them all, Captain.'

Without the slightest indication from Arora, the restaurant manager brought over another plate of piping hot kebabs and reverentially placed it before the fat man in the manner of a high priest bringing a sacrificial offering, to his god. As far as the manager was concerned, Arora saab was a big shot government employee who had benevolently rid him of the pesky policemen who, despite collecting ever increasing quantities of hafta, had insisted on eating three free meals each day. The SHO had been furious when the Havildar returned empty-handed one afternoon, but a flash of Arora's identity card had tempered his fury, and the casual mention of a few names had convinced him to diversify his palate permanently. In gratitude, the manager gave Arora heavy discounts and made sure he was always seated at the most discreet table available.

The fourth plate went down Arora's gullet and returned a satisfied burp. Sablok cringed.

'Oh! You faujis with the batons stuck up your backsides. Scrunch up your face all you want, you're paying for the meal.'

'Then I had better get my money's worth,' Sablok replied.

Even though he had spent twenty-five years in the profession, Arora performed a role at the Europe section similar to Sablok's. Like the younger man, he was comfortable where he was. Unlike Sablok, however, Arora had begun his career in intelligence. It had once been hinted to Sablok by one of his colleagues that Arora had spied on Gandhi and Nehru before independence, and those actions were to blame for his lack of authority within his own section.

Arora listened as Sablok briefed him about the Pakistani delegation.

'This is not much to go on, Captain. Did you discuss it with your superiors?'

"I did," Sablok said. He made as if to say more, then sighed and shrugged.

Arora nodded. 'I don't blame Mishra. The dhoti wallas are demanding miracles from him every day, and the poor fellow doesn't have enough money to perform them regularly. Besides, this hypothesis of yours is highly speculative.'

After a long silence, he called the manager over and ordered two cups of masala chai. Sablok slumped slightly in his seat. His leg was beginning to throb.

Arora sipped his tea, observing him. Finally, he spoke. 'What kind of help do you expect from me?'

Sablok looked up.

'The diplomat. I'm certain he's a thug. But his file at the Archives is woefully inadequate. If I could get corroboration of my suspicions about him, and perhaps some information about his activities while he was posted here…'

Arora smiled.

'This might turn out to be much ado, Captain. And even if you get confirmation, your chief may not budge. Even so, give me a few days.'

When Arora returned to his office that afternoon, he dialled an outside line and made an appointment to meet at six that evening. Just before leaving, he dispatched a cable to the Resident at The Hague.

The Hague (the Netherlands)

C. B. Malathi stepped into her office after a working brunch hosted by the Deputy Chief of Mission, a frizzy-haired diplomat of fifty who knew more about Dutch diplomacy than most of the IFS put together. She walked over to the desk and sank into the plush leather chair, the tip of her tongue feeling the warm inside of her cheeks, savouring the aftertaste of the Bordeaux that the Deputy Chief had uncorked. A few eyebrows had been raised when she accepted a glass, but she wasn't going to decline a '47 Château Cheval Blanc. For one thing, it was a gift from the French ambassador to his Indian counterpart on Independence Day and, for another, she couldn't hope to ever afford a bottle of it on her government salary. The raised eyebrows, patronising advice and whispered slander no longer fazed her. There had been many occasions early on in her career when she'd checked herself to please the fossils, but after nearly a decade's experience she had concluded that there was nothing she could do, short of quitting her job, to mollify those who took issue with her genitalia.

Sitting in the cool darkness of her office, its curtains drawn as usual, Malathi could feel warmth radiate from her face. She had nothing planned for the afternoon, and was considering going for a walk when the teletext in the corner of her office came to life in a shrill staccato that cared little for the afterglow of vintage wines, and vomited out a page of gibberish. Malathi had already retrieved a one-time pad from her safe before the machine was done, and decoded the cable within minutes.

'Three Pakistani nationals arrived at Schiphol from Rawalpindi via PIA flight PK785. Request you to identify their contacts in the Netherlands during their stay there.'

The cable gave further details and ended by advising caution.

'Caution!' Malathi muttered to herself. 'As usual, Delhi sits on its behind till the last possible moment, demands miracles, but advises caution while performing them.' She glanced at the calendar on her desk. 'The flight landed two days ago. How in god's name…Typical.'

She keyed in an encoded acknowledgement and sent it on its way with an irritated press of the button, then began gathering her thoughts. It was late afternoon by the time she had decided on pursuing two separate lines of enquiry. There was a driver at the Pakistan embassy at The Hague; perhaps he had heard or seen the visitors from Rawalpindi. Then there was that airport worker at Schiphol.

The journey to India Gate took Arora seventeen minutes in his white Fiat. Purchasing a double scoop of strawberry ice cream from a vendor near the parking lot, he walked to the vast greens near the monument, and sat on a vacant bench; moments later he was engrossed in his cone. He was halfway through the second scoop when the person he was meeting walked over and sat beside him. Forty-five years old, give or take a day, he seemed the kind of person who awoke before dawn each day to grimace painfully while running around the roads of Chanakyapuri and then swore that he enjoyed doing it.

'That looks nice,' he said, indicating Arora's cone.

'Oh! You should go and get yourself one. The vendor's over there, behind that tree,' Arora replied, then added, 'and get one more for me too—double scoop, please.'

The man returned with two cones and handed one to Arora. He had paranoid eyes that kept darting from side to side even while eating ice cream.

'Must we meet in public like this?' he asked.

'How else will people know we're star-crossed lovers,' Arora said, then laughed at his companion's disgusted expression. 'Family doing alright?'

'They're fine. You could come over for dinner instead of dragging me out of important meetings and then filling my head with horrible images.'

'I am never again visiting your house for dinner. Every time I come, your wife cooks ghiya or kaddu.'

'It might do you some good to eat healthy once in a while.'

'Go bugger yourself. With a ghiya. That's healthy too, I hear.'

'Why am I here?'

'There was a Pakistani diplomat by the name of Moraad Baksh posted to the High Commission here. What can you tell me about him?'

'When was he posted here?'

'Early '60s,' Arora replied.

'Never heard of him.'

'Find out what you can, will you?'

The other man sighed, his lips pressed together in a grimace beneath a bristly moustache now flaked with specks of cream. This wasn't the first favour Arora had asked of him, and he was sure it wouldn't be the last. Still, he owed the old man much more.

'What kind of a mess are you getting yourself into in the twilight of your career?' he asked.

Arora smiled, suggested they meet for lunch the next day, and walked away, the crunch of the cone echoing the scrunch of his footsteps on grass.

Sixteen hours after Arora's cable, Malathi wrote back: NO JOY; EFFORTS ONGOING.

Arora spent the hours before its arrival at his favourite restaurant with the friend he had met for ice cream.

'Have you joined the Mafia?' his friend asked after noticing the deference with which the staff treated Arora. The fat man dismissed the idea between gulps of syrupy lassi embellished with a dollop of malai and a strand of saffron.

'They just know I work for the government,' he added. 'Perhaps that isn't very different from being a Mafiosi from their perspective.'

'You would make a decent Godfather,' his friend replied.

'I have been told that I am the spitting image of a younger Brando,' Arora quipped to guffaws.

After the manager had served tandoori chicken and retreated out of earshot, the friend spoke: 'Baksh is a grade A thug.'

Arora felt a surge of excitement but kept it from his voice or face.

'The file was vague, mind you, and I had to ask around discreetly, to get the full picture. Don't even think about asking for a copy. Verboten! There's a term you're familiar with. Anyway, our people spotted him in '66, after the war. He was vetted much earlier when he arrived at the High Commission—as they all are—but the officers found nothing. He was fresh, you see—no history. And he lay low for the first few months at least. It was only after the war...'

The PM's death at Tashkent had set off a scramble for power among his erstwhile cabinet, Arora's friend narrated. Although the Bureau had done decent work in '65, especially compared to the debacle of '62, the brass were unhappy. They always were. They had been unable to take Lahore and so, in the era of Jai Jawaan Jai Kisaan, the blame fell upon the Bureau. Among the litany of complaints were two bombshells that rattled the cabinet. They claimed that the Bureau hadn't informed them in time about Icchogil canal, leaving 15 Division unprepared when the Pakistanis breached it. The Bureau protested, of course; it had provided precise inputs about Icchogil. The second assault came in the form of strong suspicions voiced by Army Commanders that the Pakistanis had precise knowledge, in some areas, of Indian battle plans. The implication was that a mole had escaped the Bureau's notice and buried itself somewhere in the large olive green meadow. The Bureau took exception to this too, but quietly constituted a team to dig the rodent out.

The team took back-bearings from the battle plans that field commanders felt the enemy had an awareness of. Nearly three months of painful sleuthing later, they narrowed the list of suspects down to two officers associated with the Directorate of Operations. Surveillance and a plump, juicy carrot led them to Baksh. The Bureau began quietly identifying his network in Delhi. Once they were convinced they had most of it laid bare, they rolled it up in one swoop.

'What about outside Delhi?' Arora asked.

'There was a Batman to a staff officer in one of the formations on the western front. Baksh also visited Bombay a few times. Short trips; flew out on an early morning flight, back in Delhi by nightfall.'

'Did they find out what he was up to?'

'He evaded surveillance in Bombay on all three occasions. The trips were always unexpected, and the team struggled to maintain tradecraft. By then the Bureau had had enough. The Director went to the Foreign Secretary and had Baksh declared persona non grata. The next day he returned to Islamabad, likely to a hero's welcome.'

The frown on Arora's face became severe.

'Short trips to Bombay. Do you think he was servicing an agent there? What did the Case Officer say about those trips?'

'He noted that, on each occasion, Baksh evaded surveillance near Chembur, and felt strongly that he had a high-value agent there.'

'I'd like to speak to him. Where is that Case Officer now?'

'Taken prisoner outside Dhaka in '71 and murdered.'

CHAPTER THREE

A rora left office exactly at 5 p.m. and drove to Connaught Circus. A lifetime of banking there had taught him that his bank, which was located in a lane off Parliament Street, would be deserted at that hour, so he parked in its parking lot. The security guard glanced once in his direction, then returned his attention to the music blaring from his transistor radio. Nobody suspects the obese, Arora chuckled to himself. Outside, the muggy heat of the day was yielding slowly to a soft breeze. Footpaths weren't crowded yet. Walking along Jantar Mantar, he entered an old bookstore on Connaught Lane. Diligently, he browsed each stack and shelf, bending with not a little difficulty to scrutinize the lowest shelves. The grey-bearded owner was no stranger to people who had to satisfy themselves with the fragrance and touch of someone else's books, and paragraphs read on the sly—bibliophiles caught under the crushing weight of Roti-Kapda-Makaan. These victims of a love that defied consummation reminded him of his own youth, and he never bothered them, not even those that spent the entire day reading a book or two from cover to cover.

At 6:30 p.m. Arora purchased a paperback with Matryoshka dolls on its cover, wished the owner good health, and left. Beads of sweat had adorned his upper lip, and his legs burned in complaint.

Ignoring them, he plodded on. The main attraction at Regal Cinema was Kunwara Baap, but the walls of the theatre were covered with posters for a matinee show about a call girl. He was out of breath and sweating profusely by then, and a vacant park bench opposite the cinema let him rest his weary legs. A family of four walked by, the wife studiously avoiding so much as a glance at the woman on the posters showing décolletage, and the husband sneaking a peek every few steps. Both piously shooed their children along whenever they stared. Mosquitoes had begun buzzing Arora's ears rather noisily, so when the sweat became less torrential and his breathing was no longer laboured, he stood up and walked around among early-evening shoppers and people milling about. At 7:30 p.m., he headed back to Regal Cinema, purchased a handful of salted peanuts that the street vendor wrapped in a packet made of old newsprint, and stepped into a dark corner. He spotted Sablok just as the last of the peanuts were settling into his stomach.

'Oye! Captain!' he shouted. A few heads turned in his direction, but he was paying attention to those that did not, committing their faces to memory.

Sablok walked over.

'Arora saab, imagine meeting you here.'

Both men feigned surprise. Over the next quarter hour, they ambled around making small talk, walking back and forth around Regal Cinema. At one point, when Sablok stopped to purchase salted peanuts, Arora discreetly scanned the faces around them; he was looking for people who lingered, and for other anomalies that might suggest that they were under surveillance—they weren't. Convinced, he walked over to the ticket counter, purchased two tickets to the stalls, and waved Sablok over. Inside the cinema hall, they sat in the dark near the exit and, after a few minutes, quietly slipped out into a narrow alley behind the building. A long walk and short drive later, Sablok found himself staring at a walnut wood nameplate that simply said, "J. Arora."

Inside, the living room looked disused—a stack of ironed clothes still wrapped in newsprint lay precariously balanced near the edge of the settee; the chairs handled the overflow from the bookcase; the coffee table had a heap of newspapers and magazines covering it, along with a few cups caked with dark brown residue. Every surface in the room seemed dusty, except the photos of Arora's son and wife on the wall. The large Murphy valve radio in the corner appeared to have fallen into disrepair. On their way there, they had purchased anda bhurji and kulchas. Arora collected the packets from Sablok and stepped into the kitchen. All that walking had left him famished.

'Make yourself comfortable,' he shouted from inside.

By the time Sablok had cleared a chair of books and sat down, Arora returned with food neatly served on two plates, pushed the clothes off the settee to make room for himself, and offered one plate to his guest. He half-mumbled an apology for the state of the house, clearly uncomfortable with the mess. Sablok waved it away with a platitude about long work hours. They ate in silence.

Later, after dinner, Arora brought water and ice with two freshly washed tumblers and an unopened bottle of whisky. Sablok was halfway through his first Patiala peg when Arora finally spoke about Baksh and gave Sablok a verbatim account of what he had learnt earlier that day, interspersed with contextual digressions. It was a two-drink narrative, and not once did he even hint at the identity of his source. Sablok listened carefully.

'We should requisition this file officially,' Sablok finally said. 'Can you get its serial from your source?'

He wanted to provide definitive proof to Mishra, and his approach betrayed the bureaucratic habits that had survived his exit from the army.

Arora smiled wistfully and shook his head, scrubbing his own stubble with the left hand. 'It's too late for convincing your boss,' he murmured. 'Besides, my source won't stick their neck out any further. The file's existence—should we officially ask for it—will prove embarrassing for a lot of very influential people.'

Sablok looked confused. Arora cleared it up for him with a brief history of the Wing.

'The events in that file are from just before the Wing was created from part of the Bureau—think of Prajapati creating his own wife, or Adam and his rib if you're so inclined. When the Wing came into existence in '68, all relevant files were meant to be shared between parent and child. A famed committee of three decided which were relevant. The one we seek now did not pass muster. If we somehow find its serial and send in a requisition through the Secretary, the first reaction of these three—all of whom work for the Bureau, by the way—will be to find out how we caught wind of its existence. After the hounds take back bearings from the file's history, it may take them five minutes—seven if our stars are favourable—to finger my contact. A day later they'll know about me. From that point on until we're dead and cremated, the Bureau will bugger my contact and me with a ten-foot pole wrapped in razor wire. Such a device is also known by the bland name of the Official Secrets Act of Nineteen Twenty-Three. No, we proceed without the file.'

Sablok had never seen him so animated: eyes gleaming in the light of two sixty-watt incandescents, voice spirited, and the hand not holding his glass gesturing violently. Perhaps it was the drink. Having made his argument, Arora retreated to his usual state, his eyes half closed and dull, fleshy chin resting on his chest. Sablok stared intensely at the last dregs that remained in the bottle, his mind contemplating absurd fantasies like breaking into the Bureau to retrieve what they needed. A little later, having run out of options, he found himself staring at a photograph of Arora and his wife with their son at the latter's commissioning ceremony in '62. The spymaster had been much thinner back then, and all three seemed delighted. Arora looked as proud as any father can be. When Sablok compared that to the photo of his family from his own commissioning a year later, the contrast was jarring.

'I've become addle-brained,' Arora shouted in self-recrimination, reaching for the bottle and emptying it in one gulp. His ears were a bright crimson and radiated heat. The amber burned his throat and earned a grimace. 'The operation shouldn't focus on the Pakistan Atomic Energy Commission angle at all. We'll run it through my section instead, ostensibly to uncover Baksh's network in Europe. If an old India hand makes a dash for Amsterdam, odds are he is servicing an agent. The delegation is merely a fig leaf to disguise the real objective of his trip. The scientists within the delegation would have to be investigated, of course. And if we happen to find something, well, we would have no choice but to follow the evidence, wouldn't we?'

Sablok marvelled at the elegance of the solution as Arora listed the

27

challenges he foresaw, and how they could work around them. But a clear voice of self-preservation called out to him over the din of professional admiration. The first obstacle Arora needed to overcome was getting Sablok involved in an operation run through the Europe section. Teams drawn from different parts weren't unknown within the Wing, but each member's participation was contingent on his or her section chief signing off. Sablok had a feeling Mishra wouldn't take kindly to a subordinate manoeuvring behind his back. Arora read his expression correctly.

'We could make it appear as if the information came to us from the Resident at The Hague. You'll be off the hook,' he said.

'But then I won't get to participate in the operation.'

Arora nodded. 'Maybe you could gamble on being too insignificant for your chief to really bother about,' he suggested, helpfully.

'I can't afford to lose my job,' Sablok retorted.

'You're a government servant, Captain. You couldn't lose your job even if you set out to accomplish just that. The beauty of being a public official is that the worst your boss can do to you is replace himself.'

Sablok wasn't convinced.

'Are you quite certain?'

'Of course. The worst he can do is give you nonsense work in the hope that you'll quit out of boredom. He can transfer you, but there aren't many desk jobs outside Delhi.'

'Perhaps you could call in one of your favours,' Sablok pleaded.

Arora remembered the favours he had called in to recruit Sablok into the Wing in '72. The plan had been straightforward back then: get Sablok into the Wing, have him assigned to Europe, and get him out into the field.

'Best laid plans of mice and men,' Arora muttered under his breath.

The first part had been easy, but during a particularly strenuous exercise during training—one that was designed to stress the agent's psyche to the limit—Sablok suffered a breakdown after a series of flashbacks to that afternoon in '71, and that drew attention to his mental health. The training officer would not overlook what Arora tried to convince him was a minor episode, and the best Arora could do from that point on was to get Sablok a desk job.

'Favours only go so far, Captain,' Arora sighed. He had let Sablok down once before. 'The favours I call in won't save your career from progressing slower than molasses…'

'But they may get me on the operation, right?'

'I cannot guarantee anything at this moment. The whole thing might unravel, leaving you to the tender mercies of your Chief. Do you want to go ahead with the plan and risk his displeasure?'

'I can deal with hostility,' Sablok said with a smile.

'Keep a low profile for the next few days,' Arora said as Sablok rose to leave. 'And have a little faith,' he added. 'I hear it can move mountains.'

CHAPTER FOUR

The next afternoon, Arora began leaving breadcrumbs. In a cable to the Resident in Paris, a promising young officer only recently posted there, he asked if the Resident was aware of attempts by the opposition to recruit members of the Arab community in France for the purpose of carrying out activities detrimental to India's national interests. The cable referred to communication that predated the Resident's tenure, an attempt at manufacturing proof that Sablok wasn't responsible for what would follow. An officer with greater experience, or even a green one who had had time to settle into a new post, would have either challenged the premise of such a provocatively framed question or would have dismissed it entirely. Fearing such a result, Arora piled on the pressure by mentioning in the cable that the document was being copied to the Section Chief, Europe. He took a copy of the cable, marked it to the Chief, and accidentally lost it in a file that he then locked in his own safe. The response from Paris was quick: such recruitment was a concern as the poor economic conditions of recent migrants from the Maghreb made the community ripe for religious infiltration; while activity at the Pakistani Embassy at Rue Lord Byron, Paris was not unusual, attempts to target the Banlieues could not be ruled out. It was the perfect non-answer of a government servant threatened with an urgent deadline. Arora pounced upon it, using it as a pretext to cable similar questions to Residents in other capitals in Western Europe. Each response received by him earned a follow-up that dug deeper, and by the end of the week, he had a fat stack of worrying cables.

The expected summons from the Section Chief arrived on Tuesday morning.

'Congratulations,' the Section Chief exclaimed when Arora entered his office. A large desk covered with many piles of documents occupied most of the room. The grey-haired incumbent sat leaning back on a plush leather chair behind it, his hands casually interlocked behind his head. Arora sat sheepishly before his mentor and kept his mouth shut. After subjecting the rogue analyst to an exaggerated stare, the Chief leant to the left and rested his thickly bearded cheek on his palm.

'As you are now running this section, I thought it fit to extend felicitations and then retire to Bardez as a relieved man,' Almeida said.

He then retrieved a quart of gin from a drawer and poured two drinks.

'Chief, I was about to come and brief you—'

'How considerate.'

Arora glanced at his wristwatch before accepting a glass.

'Unless you have suddenly found religion after debauching yourself your entire life, Jugs, do not dare raise an eyebrow. This is an anti-malarial prophylactic, nothing more. Down the hatch!' After a satisfying gulp, he continued, 'Now, what in god's name possessed you?'

Arora explained, between sips, that he had been trying to outline the extent of the ISI's infiltration of Europe as an academic exercise, a primer of sorts for new recruits.

'Until I explicitly ask for the service, do not presume to blow smoke up my derrière.'

Finishing the rest of his drink in one gulp, Arora quietly extended his glass for a refill. The older man obliged, then told him to stop stalling.

'This is your last drink, one way or another. Speak up before it is gone.'

'Jilani Khan's thugs are escalating their activities in a West European country, sir. A delegation of Pakistani scientists flew there last week, chaperoned by one of those thugs, a career villain who spent more years here in Delhi in the '50s and '60s than either of us did.'

'Providing security,' Almeida reasoned.

'Would you send me on a trip to Hong Kong to provide security? Since when are India hands recycled to Europe? This chap isn't a foot soldier, believe me. He ran networks here that spread from the MoD to field formations. And those are just the ones we know about. He also made frequent and short visits to Bombay, but managed to evade surveillance each time.'

'Where in Bombay?'

'The team lost him in Chembur twice, and once at Antop Hill.'

'Trombay!'

Arora nodded vigorously.

'These Pakistani scientists…'

'A nuclear engineer and a physicist, Chief, from their Atomic Energy Commission,' Arora answered. 'They flew to Schiphol on PIA. It was a hastily planned trip: they flew First Class because Economy and Business were overbooked. To the best of my knowledge, they have not linked up with their Resident at The Hague. I know the Netherlands isn't my assignment, but—'

'Bugger that. Why didn't you come to me directly instead of stomping all over with solicitous cables?'

'We didn't receive the intelligence directly. It came to us from the Pakistan section illicitly. Fruit of the forbidden tree, sir.'

Almeida winced. 'Please leave the Biblical references to me. Who received the inputs, and what was the source?'

Arora studiously examined the dregs of his gin.

Almeida gave him a hard look. 'You're asking me to go toe to toe with a section three times our size and so flush with resources their miscellaneous expenses dwarf our operational budget. I won't even contemplate such a reckless act unless you give me every detail.'

'A cable from someone at the embassy in Islamabad. He recruited a PIA stewardess, and she gave him the information. An analyst at the Pakistan section by the name of Sablok caught it.'

'Caught it? Like Syphilis? Never mind. I am more concerned with whom he gave it to. What did he do when he realised its import? Surely he did not bring it straight to Jugs Arora, spymaster extraordinaire.

Please tell me you are not running a network inside our own Pakistan section because that is one headache I would rather do without.'

'Captain Sablok took the cable to his Section Chief after gathering contextual information. His arguments were heard, but his request was denied. So he reached out to me. He thought if he could only get substantial corroboration about the thug, then perhaps his chief would reconsider. After he requested me, I—'

'Jugs, I really do not want to hear about you wheedling information from our former masters lest they call me to testify at your trial. Why did his Chief decline permission? Surely with all the money the Secretary keeps showering their section with, he could afford an indulgence or two.'

'Something brewing in Bangladesh, boss. All available resources are being directed there.'

'Again? Ominous. Presumably, you want me to pick up the slack. Make your case,' Almeida said.

'In '71, sir, we overwhelmed them, split them in two. Earlier this year we detonated an atom bomb of our own. The Pakistani establishment has to be paranoid to the point of psychosis right now. And with someone as aggressive as Bhutto leading them...Look, they're outnumbered and terrified of our armoured columns piercing deep into the heart of Punjab. They can't purchase enough tanks or artillery to match us. So what else is left? They'll have learned from NATO's mad plans for the Fulda Gap, I guarantee it. Those plans to stop a Soviet armoured offensive by dropping atom bombs were common knowledge in Berlin when I was posted there. There is no reason to assume Bhutto won't try everything he can to get his hands on the bomb. Now consider the thug: he spent a decade in India, servicing multiple networks; he took a close interest in the part of Bombay that houses our atomic programme. Is it so far-fetched that he might have recruited someone there? Viewed against this backdrop, the delegation to Schiphol doesn't seem very innocent, does it? And they're in Europe, our neck of the woods. Why should we hesitate?'

After a few minutes of reflection, during which Arora downed his third drink and wiped the sweat from his forehead, Almeida appeared to have made up his mind.

'I will authorise a limited operation. Pay close attention to the word "limited", Jugs. You can investigate the European end of this drama, but under no circumstances are you to even dream about any action on Pakistani territory. Keep it low key, and make sure the Pakistan section does not catch wind of it. I do not want to dance with that bear.'

Arora did not budge. His lack of fawning gratitude annoyed Almeida.

'Anything else?' he asked.

After a moment's consideration and a deep breath, Arora answered, 'I just recalled that incident in Berlin. It was in '63, I think. The details are a bit hazy now, sir, but—'

'Bloody hell, Arora, what do you want?'

'The analyst that brought the cable to my attention: Captain Sablok. I'd like him on my team for this operation, sir.'

'Why does that name sound familiar to me, Jugs?'

'I recruited him, sir.'

'Oh, wonderful! Not only will Mishra dislike the interference, he will be convinced you are recruiting agents and planting them in his section to keep tabs on him. And since you report to me, he will devote his considerable talents to taking me apart. No can do, Arora babu. Captain Sablok stays where he is.'

'Please hear me out, sir,' Arora persisted. 'Despite all these breadcrumbs, the moment the operation yields product and we need good people in the Pakistan section, their Section Chief will put two and two together and skewer Sablok for going behind his back—'

'As would I, in similar circumstances.'

'Skewer someone for doing the right thing for the country?'

'That last part remains to be seen.'

'Sablok isn't some Stephen's graduate who's still wet behind the ears, sir. He nearly won the Sword of Honour at Doon, then served with my son in '65. Walked into a minefield in broad daylight because the armoured column behind him needed a path through it. In '71, when the Wing sought Bengali speaking soldiers, he volunteered and led repeated raids deep into Sylhet long before the army had mobilised, providing crucial support to Osmani's men and performing terrain reconnaissance. For his efforts, the Pakistanis gifted him seven fragments of an anti-personnel landmine, one of which remains, to this day, half an inch from his femoral artery. When the doctors told him to live with it, he asked to have the whole leg amputated to keep his career alive. This is the sort of stuff he is made of, sir. He deserves better.'

'We are not a humanitarian organisation.'

'No, sir. That we are not. We recruit agents—often the scum of the earth—and we use them. But even then, once they've outlived their use to us, we do our best to keep our end of the bargain.'

'Make do without. If the hammer falls on him, we will do what we can for him.'

There was a sense of the absolute in Almeida's rejection. Arora sat contemplating the essence of the years he had surrendered at the altar of the state. The conflicted distaste of the '40s, the short-lived euphoria of independence, the professional mortification that followed. Through it all, he had clung on, tenaciously hoping for a better tomorrow while they kicked him around for menial work. Europe had been a new beginning, and he had greedily grabbed the lifeline that the man now refusing his requests had thrown him. When his wife's heart gave up after an LMG nest cut up their only son in '65, all hope had been snuffed out for him. The days since then bled into each other like an improperly painted watercolour. Few remained now, and he would endure them one way or another. His eyes refused to meet Almeida's.

'I'm sorry, sir. I will not make do without,' he said, staring down at his own feet.

The older man had taken pity on him once when nobody else would touch him with a ten-foot pole. He felt sorry for him once more.

'All the favours you could have asked for, and you demand this pound of flesh instead,' he said, his old head cocked to the left. 'Let me see what I can do.'

A week later, Mishra sent for Sablok.

'I underestimated your abilities, Captain Sablok,' he said, raising his eyebrows as he handed Sablok the orders sanctioning the latter's secondment to the Europe section.

Sablok kept his expression neutral as he scanned the single-page document, right down to the familiar jagged peaks of the signature etched in Mishra's arthritic hand. 'I'll do my best to deliver whatever it is they need from me, sir.'

'I hope, for your own sake, that you do, Captain; I'm not the one sticking my neck out here. Someone over there pulled a lot of strings to get you this opportunity. Don't screw it up.'

Sablok assured him that he wouldn't, then asked if he might use resources in Pakistan, should the operation demand it.

'If your crusade reaches a point where action is needed in Pakistan, I suspect our section will already be deeply involved. Till then you may direct your requests to my office.'

They shook hands, and that was it. Sablok felt a slow smile appear on his face as he stepped out of the office, clutching the envelope. That feeling lasted till he returned home that evening, whereupon it gave way to an amorphous sense of dread that could only be propitiated with half a bottle.

A small room on the second floor of Main, finagled by Arora after throwing Almeida's weight around, formed their operational HQ. It was distinguished by two desks, a safe, a dirty window, and a persistent, musty odour. A telephone line materialised eventually, as did a teletext machine. Spending most of the next two weeks in the Archives digging deeper into Pakistan's atomic energy bureaucracy, Sablok saw little of that small room. When details became too technical for him, which happened depressingly early into the effort, he wrote to Mishra. The Pakistan section of the Wing had worked closely with India's own scientists to keep the weapons programme secure and quiet in the '60s and '70s, and Sablok hoped the relationships forged then had survived. The innocuous request was also a good way to check if Mishra's half-hearted consent to supporting the operation was sincere. The reply arrived two days later, pointing him in the direction of a physicist from BARC who was currently on deputation to the Prime Minister's Office in Delhi.

Arora's approach was a bit more hands on. Badgering analysts who specialised in matters concerning Belgium and the Netherlands, he demanded to know if Dutch population registers could possibly be used to identify a particular immigrant. When they complained that it wasn't feasible, he browbeat them in Almeida's name and tasked them with finding a way to identify Pakistani immigrants somewhere around Amsterdam. The brief he gave them was limited and contained no details; they had to come up with an approach before he read them into the operation.

36

The first breakthrough arrived in the second week of October in the form of a cable from the Resident at The Hague. C. B. Malathi wrote that Sultan Mahmood, Moraad Baksh, and Nadeem Khan—the Pakistani delegation she had been asked to track—had flown back to Karachi just twenty-four hours after their arrival at Schiphol. A copy of the flight manifest was on its way to Delhi via diplomatic pouch. Their return appeared pre-planned as the tickets had been booked at the same time as the Karachi-Schiphol tickets. She also mentioned that they had travelled to the airport by taxi and that the driver was being identified. But considering how much time had elapsed, she did not expect to learn much from him. The cable ended by asking if Arora's enquiries had been exploratory in nature.

Arora had Sablok draft a reply: 'The enquiries are now operational,' it began, before delving into the defining parameters of the operation. It sought to know if the Resident could procure Dutch immigration records—inbound ones—for further analysis in India. Sablok wanted to add a note of caution regarding the class of thugs she was dealing with, but Arora advised against it.

'Don't patronise her. She's better at the job than both of us put together.'

They sent the cable at 4 pm. The reply came seven minutes later: 'NOT POSSIBLE.'

It was fresh in Sablok's mind when he rode to South Block that evening with an extensive list of questions. He was supposed to meet Anil Saha, the contact his former boss had recommended. Expecting a more stereotypical appearance, he started when a tall, lean man with short cropped hair approached him in the lobby and asked if he was Captain Sablok. The physicist was dressed sharp in formals and appeared to have perfect eyesight. Sablok did not have prior clearance to visit other parts of the huge complex, so Saha found an empty sofa in the lobby.

'This isn't really an interview. I'm just trying to understand aspects of your profession. My boss told me to seek your help,' Sablok said.

'Of course, Captain. But, to be honest, the Army has never shown much interest in what we do. Why the change of heart, if I may ask?'

Sablok explained that he no longer worked for the Army, and evaded Saha's follow-up by stating that they both reported to the PMO, in a way. Saha had been ordered to meet Captain Sablok by someone many rungs above him, so he accepted the evasion and began answering Sablok's questions.

Towards the end, Sablok asked Saha his opinion about Pakistan's attempts at acquiring a nuclear weapon. After a long monologue, half of which Sablok thought he may be able to grasp only after a few years of intensive study, Saha opined that the major roadblocks were technological. Manufacturing the required components was tough, and he doubted if they had the expertise to perfect explosive lenses and timing circuits for an implosion-type device which used Plutonium as fuel. The other approach would be to build a simple gun-type bomb, but that required enriched Uranium.

'Enrichment is a bastard of a process, Captain,' he added. 'They don't have the know-how to go down that route. And besides, the French are already building them a Plutonium reprocessing plant. They'll have so much weapons grade Plutonium in a few years that they won't even have to think about enriching Uranium.'

The consensus among his peers, he reported, was that Pakistan would not be able to manufacture a device on its own in the foreseeable future.

'If Bhutto made you head of their programme, what kind of scientists would you hire?' Sablok asked.

'I wouldn't. They have plenty of good physicists. I would hire engineers, preferably those with experience with nuclear weapons. And I'd ask them to bring advanced tools with them in suitcases.'

'These tools fit in suitcases?' Sablok asked, the hair on his arms rising.

'Just kidding, Captain,' Saha said, with a chuckle. 'The tools are very large. They fill up factories worth of space.'

Later, as he bid Saha goodbye, Sablok asked if he would mind answering more questions in the future, preferably without the need to go up and down their respective chains of command.

'Certainly. Provided you tell me for whom you work.'

CHAPTER FIVE

In November, as clothing became thicker and the sky turned a deeper shade of blue, each passing non-productive day brought Arora's arteries closer to rupture.

They had begun by trying to understand what they were up against, trying to imagine the kind of operation that the ISI would run.

'Stealing nuclear secrets from another country, even an ally, is a dangerous proposition. There are few things governments are as paranoid about protecting as nuclear secrets,' Arora reasoned. 'If they're caught trying to steal them, the diplomatic fallout will be tremendous. Not to mention the economic and military sanctions Western Europe and America will clobber them with.'

It was Sablok's first intelligence operation. Keenly aware of his own inexperience, he stayed quiet and let Arora continue thinking out loud.

'Now I'm not suggesting, Captain, that they aren't capable of bold moves. They're insulated from political oversight, and answer only to 'Pindi. They aren't incapable of gambling, and often succeed when they do. But the risks are too high this time. They will be cautious. They will be conservative. The asset will be someone who has a deep bond with Pakistan, someone whose loyalty to the Pakistan state wouldn't be as questionable as, say, that of a white European. Besides, if they had to send two experts, it could be to validate the authenticity of the asset or his claims. That would mean it was the asset who approached them first, not the other way around. If I were a betting man, I would wager my pension that this asset is a Pakistani immigrant. All we have to do is find him.'

But finding that Pakistani immigrant was proving difficult and frustrating.

The analysts he had bullied came back and advised Arora that the only way to get their hands on a list of all Pakistanis in the Netherlands was by formally requesting the Dutch domestic spooks, the BVD.

'What piercing insight!' Arora grumbled to Sablok. 'If only more intelligence agencies would just cooperate with their rivals instead of indulging in all the usual cloak-and-dagger nonsense.'

Given India's growing proximity to the USSR, especially after the latter's famous veto in favour of India in the UN Security Council in '71, seeking help from the BVD against the Pakistanis was a nonstarter. His other great hope had been Malathi's pursuit of the taxi driver, but after a few weeks without success, it had become clear that salvation lay not in that direction. Like the ambient temperature outside, Arora could feel the beginning of a chill whenever he spoke with Almeida about the operation. The questions asked of him were becoming perfunctory, and the pressure to deliver product became Vetala to Arora's Vikramaditya.

In desperation, he cabled Malathi and asked if she had contacts within the BVD who might be persuaded to trade the records that the Wing sought. For lack of any other lead, he was fixated on the Dutch immigration records.

Malathi's response was swift: 'It would take months to process lakhs of records even with a dedicated team of analysts, and by then the outcome may no longer matter. I see no value in pursuing this line of enquiry, especially given the heightened risk of exposing the entire operation to the BVD. If the BVD freezes us out, the Wing would be effectively blind to Pakistani proliferation in the Netherlands. In any case, I do not have contacts capable of executing this, nor do I have the product to trade for it.'

Arora was resting his head on the desk, nursing a headache induced by the reply when Sablok stepped in. He glanced at the message.

'Well, she's not wrong, sir.'

Arora looked up, his eyes bloodshot and bathed in agony.

'I mean, we don't have a team of analysts to do our bidding. And it will take a lot of time to translate hundreds of thousands of Dutch records and then analyse them. Speaking of which, how do you plan to ferret out our chap from all those other Pakistanis in Amsterdam?'

'My astrologer keeps this parrot,' Arora replied. 'Beautiful plumage, and a beak redder than Romy Schneider's lips. I'm told that bird excels at picking out cards.'

Sablok did not know who Romy Schneider was, but, guessing it must be a woman, he laughed politely. Arora stared impassively at him for a few moments before speaking again: 'Gender, education, employer; bread and butter analysis, Captain. But we can't do that until we have information, and it appears we are no longer capable of acquiring any. In my day we infiltrated embassies; now we can't even steal documents from bureaucrats.'

Sablok cleared his throat discreetly and waited for the rant to peter out. 'What kind of education would you filter for?' he asked.

'Nuclear physics, I suppose,' Arora replied in a gruff voice. 'I haven't given much thought to it yet.'

'I met an expert a few days ago to get clarifications about nuclear bombs,' Sablok said. 'At the end, I asked what he would do if Bhutto made him the head of their weapons programme.'

'You asked what?' Arora exclaimed, his face contorted in surprise.

'Don't worry. He works at the PMO, and—'

'And that's where half the leaks come from, Captain. What were you thinking?'

'Hear me out, sir. He worked on our own bomb. My Section Chief knew him from back then. Mishra told me to contact him if I needed answers. That question was hypothetical. I haven't said anything about the operation. But he seemed well informed about the Pakistani programme.'

'Are you certain that you did not let any details slip?' Arora finally asked after many moments of consideration. Sablok assured him he had not.

'He said they have enough physicists. It is capable engineers that they lack,' Sablok added.

41

'What kind of engineers?'

'He did not say, and I did not pursue it because I did not want to tip our hand.'

That evening, Arora sought permission to consult an expert. A little before 10 p.m., Almeida called Arora in to discuss the request. He was in a dark mood after one of his frequent run-ins with the administration and began by pointedly asking about the status of the operation, scoffing at Arora's answer, and finally wondering aloud if this request wasn't a gambit to cover up an utter lack of progress. Arora cautiously explained that the complicated and esoteric nature of the topic was proving to be a handful. An expert—a nuclear physicist—would be very helpful in making sure they were looking for the right person.

'I thought you brought that Sablok chap for precisely that reason.' Almeida was in an unreasonable frame of mind.

'He's an analyst, Chief. He's supposed to know what questions to ask, not all their answers. It is unfair to expect doctorate-level knowledge.'

'Unfair? Do not broach the topic of fairness with me, Jugs. I had to eat what those delightful Americans so colourfully call a shit sandwich, and I had to praise Mishra for its flavour and texture because you insisted on that analyst. And after all that, Mishra gets an open channel into the heart of our operation. When the time is right, he will generously volunteer to carry it to its logical conclusion because it will inevitably lead into that execrable land of pure shit which he believes is his fief, and if you screw the operation up before that, well, he gets to keep his knotty hands clean. I am buggered either way, all thanks to your quest for fairness.'

'And yours, sir,' Arora replied, his tone soothing and conciliatory. Almeida stared at him.

'My compassion is finite,' he finally said. 'You have two months to show me progress. Make sure this Saha fellow is subjected to a background check. And find somewhere else to debrief him. I do not want him in our compound.'

It took the bureau all of three days to clear Saha. Arora suspected that they had recycled a previous background check. Two days later, Almeida's permission—which had now taken the form of a letter from the PMO—snaked its way through the DAE's labyrinths and landed on Saha's supervisor's desk. Almeida's diktat about not using the Wing's facilities created logistical complications, though. It took Sablok's generous offer of the use of his apartment near ISBT to resolve them.

Late in the evening of the nineteenth of November, Arora drove to the PMO to ferry Saha to Civil Lines. The air was unusually dusty for the season, and Arora had to stop twice to clean his windscreen with a cloth, the wipers having long given up on the task. His quiet manner and the cloak-and-dagger routine of driving to an unknown location for a consult forestalled any thoughts of casual conversation that Saha might have entertained, and the latter sat looking out of the window at cycles, scooters, cycle rickshaws, and horse tongas. Lambrettas and Vespa scooters lined either side of Sablok's lane, leaving barely enough room for two adults to walk abreast. Arora parked on the main street near its entrance, blocking a now closed ration shop, and the two of them walked to Sablok's apartment. Most residents were already asleep, their windows dark and shuttered tight against the dust and cold. Sablok was down two pegs, the maintenance dose for his leg, when they knocked on the door. Saha visibly relaxed when he saw the familiar face. Once inside, Arora handed Saha three documents and swore him to secrecy in such a perfunctory and underwhelming manner that the physicist casually signed and returned them after the briefest glance through each one. Sablok offered them both a drink; Saha declined.

Arora accepted a large peg and drank deep before asking Saha to describe his job in '66. Saha shifted in his chair and crossed his arms, uncrossed them a moment later, then, making up his mind, crossed them once more. Between '64 and '69, he was a student at Trinity College in Dublin, he told them. In '66 he was pursuing a doctorate there. Sablok was suitably impressed, but Arora barely even reacted beyond slowly scribbling into a notepad.

'It must have been a rigorous programme. I've heard Trinity is a very prestigious institution,' he said in the flat tone of a mediocre newsreader.

Saha nodded, prompting some more scribbling.

'Did you take any vacations?'

Another nod, not worth ink on paper, apparently.

'Were you on vacation in India between July and September '66?'

'I don't remember. It was a decade ago.'

'Eight years ago,' Arora corrected him.

'Eight years, then. Look, I was told you wanted my help,' Saha replied, his voice shaking almost imperceptibly; his gaze remained fixed on Sablok. 'Fascinating as my vacations are, I fail to see the relevance.'

Arora ignored the sarcasm and handed him a photograph of a man in a suit. 'Have you ever met this man?'

Saha shook his head.

'Are you sure?'

He was. It yielded a sentence or two scrawled on the notepad.

'Now think back to '66, doctor. We cannot proceed until you remember if you visited India between July and September of that year.'

'We are just being cautious,' Sablok added, earning a glare from Arora.

After a minute, Saha's face lit up in realisation.

'I did travel to India for two weeks in September. Sometime around the tenth. My sister got married on that day.'

Arora scribbled again. They could all hear the violence of the nib scraping against paper this time.

'And did you travel to Bombay on that trip? To meet friends, perhaps?'

'I had never been to Bombay before I began working at Trombay, sir. Why would I have friends there?'

'When did you join BARC, doctor?' Arora asked.

'October of '69, after completing my PhD in—'

'That's alright. We wouldn't understand it anyway,' Arora said, his pen flying across the notepad. He handed the notepad to Sablok, walked to the window and retrieved a pack of cigarettes from his shirt pocket.

'As long as you don't mind, Captain,' he said.

Sablok waved his assent, then disappeared into the bedroom with Arora's notes. Saha heard the faint, metallic sound of a telephone dial. He would have liked to listen in on the conversation that followed, but Arora called him over to the window and offered him a light. His hand shook slightly as he held the tip of the cigarette in the flame of a burning match. The first drags calmed his nerves a bit, even though he continued to sweat through his vest and shirt.

'Where did you grow up, doctor?' Arora asked.

'First of all, I'm not a doctor. And why are you interrogating me?'

Arora laughed, choking as smoke rushed out of his lungs. The coughing fit that followed brought tears to his eyes.

'Think of it as a background check,' he said, wiping his eyes. The smoke still bothered his throat, so he hawked phlegm and spat it on the road below, where it mingled with overflowing sewer water. 'If your answers cannot be verified, we'll drive you back to your guest house, and you won't see either of us ever again. Nothing more. I only asked about your childhood because you're hardly what one expects when one thinks of an accomplished scientist.'

Saha smiled, tentatively.

'Perhaps you expected unkempt grey hair?'

Arora nodded.

'You would be surprised at how many of us are normal,' Saha said.

'There is nothing ordinary about a person who chooses to indulge in calculus every day,' Arora quipped.

'Says the spy,' Saha replied.

Just then Sablok walked back into the room.

'The details check out,' he said.

Arora flicked the half-smoked cigarette out of the window. It landed in the sewage water with a faint hiss. Returning to his seat and drink, he said, 'Whenever you're ready.'

For the next half hour, they gave Saha a scrubbed overview, omitting names, vaguely alluding to dates, and mentioning a different European country. Then they asked him if he could help identify the person the Pakistanis had approached for clandestine assistance with their nuclear weapons programme.

'I really have no experience with this sort of a thing,' Saha said. 'Although, if you're asking for my assistance, you have already exhausted your usual methods, I suppose.'

'Exhausted is a strong word,' Sablok replied. 'Let's just say that we feel your insights will help us find him sooner rather than later.'

'And you're sure that they're after just one person, not a team?' Saha asked after a bit of thought.

'At the moment we are not certain of anything,' Sablok replied.

Arora jumped in before Sablok could continue. 'But it is safe to assume that they have approached an individual. I won't bother you with tedious details.'

Sablok wasn't convinced but chose to defer to Arora's judgement.

'And are you confident that the person we are looking for is a Pakistani?' Saha asked.

'It would be quite unlike the ISI to attempt a naked approach on a European. They would be wary of annoying their patrons,' Arora answered.

Saha nodded, bummed another smoke from Arora, and thought the situation through, puffing away at the window. The sound of a middle-aged woman shouting somewhere in the distance broke into his reverie. He couldn't see her in the dark, though, and after a minute of searching, he returned to the sofa. Sablok got up and shut the windows.

'As I mentioned to Captain Sablok the last time we met,' Saha began, 'The Pakistanis will be on the lookout for someone who can help them with designing or constructing the bomb. Of the two, I think they're capable of the former on their own. But building the bomb is another matter. They don't have the engineering capabilities to pull it off.'

Arora asked if Saha would be willing to bet his life on the hunch that the person approached was an engineer.

'If not an engineer by education, he is almost certain to be working on the engineering side of the nuclear industry. Look, they already have absolute giants like Abdus Salam working on the theory and design side. Unless they're recruiting Oppenheimer himself, I just don't see how hiring another physicist would make much of a difference.'

'There's always the possibility that they are not hiring this person, but using him to steal from the Europeans,' Sablok pointed out.

'It won't help much to steal documents and the like. They cannot build the machines required to construct the various components of the bomb, and after our test at Pokhran, no sane nation will give those machines to another South Asian country. There is one aspect that bothers me, though. Why did they send two scientists to recruit him?' Saha wondered.

'We have been pondering over that ourselves,' Arora said. 'Either the two scientists know the person being approached and were there as intermediaries performing introductions, or they were there to evaluate his ability to deliver. I don't give much weight to the first possibility: a phone call or letter would serve the purpose just as well. And why two scientists?'

'One of the two is an engineer,' Sablok corrected them both.

'But if they wanted to evaluate his ability, couldn't they ask him to provide a sample, a copy of some critical document, and have it analysed in Pakistan?'

Arora conceded that they did not have a clear explanation for this behaviour.

'If it helps doc— Mr Saha, the Pakistanis sent an engineer who has worked on their Karachi reactor. You mentioned that engineering is their weakness. Perhaps this might not be a coincidence,' he added.

'I'd like to perform a thought experiment, if you don't mind,' Saha said. 'What would prompt you to take me with you to Europe for meeting an Indian who might be of use to our nuclear weapons programme?'

Arora sat silently for a while, working out various possibilities. It couldn't be because he needed help with the jargon—that could be handled from the embassy. If he were approaching a potential recruit, he would do all that he could to avoid involving a third person, someone not familiar with tradecraft. The risks were just not worth it. Unless...

'Personally, I would do all I could to avoid something like that. There's too great a chance of compromising the approach one way or another. Perhaps the only reason I would even consider such a move would be if the target made extraordinary claims. It has happened before. Some people have an exaggerated opinion of their own capabilities, others just like to boast. If the target claimed, for example, that he had the exact knowledge that we badly needed, and if I wasn't capable of assessing it myself, I may consider bringing an expert along,' Arora said.

'Even if we assume that this is the reason, it doesn't help us identify the target,' Sablok complained. He saw little value in the digression.

'Perhaps not, Captain. But if we do end up with a bunch of suspects, it might help validate them. For example, an engineer employed by, say, a firm that manufactures piping for cooling a reactor cannot possibly have extraordinary insight into the manufacturing of explosive lenses,' Saha replied. 'I'm almost convinced that the person is an engineer. He could be employed in the nuclear industry, either in a corporation or a government laboratory. Or has worked for such an organization at some point in time. Certain to have studied somewhere in Europe; they wouldn't hire someone from Government College, Lahore.'

'In that case, should we begin with European universities?' Arora asked. 'What disciplines should we look into?'

'I can give you a list tomorrow,' Saha replied.

'Take all the time you want, but we need that list before you leave this room.'

By the time Saha had gone over disciplines instrumental in building a nuclear weapon with Arora and Sablok and had written them down in the form of an annotated list, it was well past midnight and Delhi was asleep. The spooks thanked him and saw him off at his guest house, bidding him a good night with a gentle reminder about the Official Secrets Act.

CHAPTER SIX

Driving through Connaught Circus on the way back from Saha's guest house, Sablok turned to Arora and asked the question that had been niggling at him.

'If Pakistan is as far behind as everyone assures us, wouldn't they need more than one person to make meaningful progress? You saw the list of disciplines: electrical engineering, chemistry, mechanical engineering, metallurgy, explosives…The list goes on. How could one agent yield product related to more than one of those, unless he was sitting in some European government laboratory with access to each and every aspect of their weapons programme?'

The thought was outlandish. If a European government laboratory dealing with nuclear weapons had been that careless with security, there was little preventing Pakistan from arming itself in short order. Arora glanced at his watch and drove on. The railway station was an island of life in the tomblike city at 3 a.m. He stopped directly opposite a tea stall, and they sipped large glasses of sweet tea to wash away the whisky occluding their minds. There was work to be done.

At Main, they drafted a cable asking Malathi to obtain records of Pakistani alumni of Dutch Universities. The cable included a list of disciplines they were primarily concerned with. It also carried instructions to conduct the investigation at arms' length and asked for weekly updates. It would have been easier for Malathi to send an IFS underling to each University, but Arora was worried University administrators would feel compelled to inform Dutch authorities about any official requests from a foreign government. He took the final draft to Almeida's office at 6:30 a.m., intercepted him as he arrived after an early breakfast, and followed him in before Almeida's assistant could block him.

'The clock is ticking,' Almeida said grimly, when Arora briefed him.

'Then I had best run,' Arora quipped. 'With your approval, of course, sir.'

'You, and run? Now that's a spectacle I would pay good money to watch,' Almeida remarked, as he authorised the request and provided the code to send the cable.

Five minutes later, the cable was sent and Arora was on his way to Connaught Place with Sablok. At Madras Coffee House, Arora inhaled deeply, taking in the thick aroma of freshly cooked sambhar, and promptly ordered breakfast and filter coffee for both.

'If this doesn't work, the operation is dead,' he said, fidgeting on the olive-green cushion of his seat.

Sablok nodded, stifling a yawn. A lifetime ago, sleep deprivation had been a regular part of daily life, but the ability to shrug it off and bash on had withered away at the desk.

'And you're right, Captain. They will eventually need a network. But every network begins with a single individual and, until we identify the man Mahmood interviewed, we cannot pursue the network he may be building for them. I have a gut feeling this mystery person in Amsterdam is the principal. Finding him will help unravel the web they're spinning. Till then we wait.'

The Hague (the Netherlands)

Around 7 a.m. at The Hague, in her first-floor office on a narrow, tree-lined street, Malathi read the cable and winced. The directive to conduct the investigation at arm's length made a simple, four-day exercise orders of magnitude more tedious. Arora's operation was beginning to annoy her, stealing her attention away from other areas that were already yielding product. The authorising code was Almeida's, though; she had verified it twice. So there was no question of ignoring the special instructions. She had no choice but to deploy one of her agents and risk exposure. After the '69 protests at Tilburg, mainly by students and faculty suspected to be influenced by communists, the BVD had ramped up surveillance and infiltration of student bodies at most Dutch universities. The thought of sending one of her established agents into such an environment worried her. The BVD likely knew who she was, but there was nothing to suggest that they had identified her networks. If they discovered one of her regulars, given enough time and resources—and the BVD lacked for neither—they would be able to roll up the network to which the regular belonged. All for a few public records. No, it would have to be Pieter. Malathi had recently recruited the middle-aged manager at one of the oldest Dutch engineering firms with the intention of building a new network around him. He was well placed to provide glimpses into Dutch industry and Malathi had kept him isolated from her regulars, most of whom were bureaucrats who yielded product on security and foreign policy. The information he would need to get was low grade. Even if the BVD sniffed him out, the worst that could happen was a slap on the wrist.

At 9 a.m., she walked along Jacob Catslaan to Carnegieplien, stopping at a public phone outside the International Court of Justice. A young journalist, blond and tall with a scruffy red-orange beard, was using the phone to animatedly brief his editor about New Zealand's case against France. From the biting invective he deployed, Malathi deduced that his views were only marginally to the right of Baader and Meinhof. He expended considerable effort in trying to impress upon his editor the need for the newspaper, in particular, and Germany, as a whole, to denounce nuclear weapons. While rambling into the handset, he turned, noticed Malathi standing five feet away and smiled, his eyes lingering. She caught a whiff of beer and cigarettes. When he hung up, he promptly made a pass at her.

She smiled back, then loudly replied 'Ich bin lesbich' to the tittering amusement of a couple of bystanders. The journalist's face reddened to match his beard and he slunk away.

She called a firm in Utrecht and asked for Sven Jansen.

'My father knew him during the war,' she added in fluent Dutch.

'I'm afraid he retired a few years ago,' came the reply.

She asked if he had left a forwarding address.

'Father wrote him a letter, and I was really hoping to take it to him,' she added.

The man on the other end offered to make enquiries with personnel and suggested that she post the letter to their office, mentioning his name on the envelope.

'Actually, I'll be in Utrecht later today. Can I hand it over in person?'

They agreed to meet later that day near the Stadskasteel Oudaen, and she thanked him for his help. Back at the embassy, she spent a few hours in preparation. After reading the cable carefully a few times to make sure there weren't any hidden surprises, she typed out a brief for Pieter. It was vague enough to bore the casual reader, an effect amplified by the fact that it began with a one-paragraph overview of the horse tranquiliser that was the government of India's education policy. The next two paragraphs explained the Indian embassy's wish to evaluate the suitability of Dutch universities for Indian students and hinted that India was keen to establish exchange programmes and a chair of studies or two. The experiences of South Asians who had studied in the Netherlands would influence the government's decision. She placed the brief in an envelope marked as a diplomatic bag and affixed the embassy's seal. Even if the BVD seized it, which they wouldn't be foolish enough to do, the letter itself was innocuous. She consulted maps of Utrecht and identified the route to take. Finally, after withdrawing two thousand guilders from the safe, she set off.

The drive along the A12 was uneventful. She missed the third exit onto Biltstraat and drove around De Voorveldse Polden a few times, but time for such tactical detours had been budgeted. There didn't appear to be a tail on her. The signboard that announced the castle before it came into view also proclaimed that it was owned by Veritas. When she saw the actual stone building, she couldn't stop herself from comparing it to Gingee. The contrast was absurd and made her chuckle. Roofs and trees were covered in snow and the wind bit into her delicate features as she walked south along the bank of the canal. A narrow street took her west, to an open square that might have been a market. Most of the city had surrendered to the weather and retreated indoors, but a few brave souls milled about. Malathi walked with a sense of purpose, but took frequent pauses, retraced her steps every once in a while, and ducked into a couple of cafes to ask for directions. At 3:30 pm, she noticed a snow-haired man following her and walked into a cafe she had scoped out earlier. There was nobody in there except for the staff, who did not show too much enthusiasm at her arrival. She sat at the back, facing the entrance, and asked for a cup of hot chocolate. The man entered, noticed her, averted his gaze quickly, and sat at a table near the door. She remained where she was and kept a wary eye on the door. She wasn't about to rush into the meeting after the charade she had gone through over the telephone that morning, and the countermeasures she had taken before finally entering the café. If Pieter was under surveillance, she would wait and let the agent following him make the first move. After perusing the menu, Pieter ordered a glass of Zopie. Nobody else entered the café. Malathi waited a good twenty minutes before pretending to notice and recognise Pieter. She walked over to his table with her half-empty cup.

Pieter was tall—six feet, give or take—and looked like he might have been a footballer once. His paunch, though, spoke of a bitter separation from the sport, as did his pallor. Deep lines flanked his pendulous, pear-shaped nose, and fine wrinkles spread from the outer corners of his eyes like cracks on a window. The creases acquired prominence when he smiled at her. The empty tables around them meant that they didn't need to keep up pretences. Malathi let him read the brief while warily watching the door. When he was done, she returned it to the diplomatic bag and, despite having done this countless times, sat back in her chair a bit easier.

'This should be simple,' he said.

The waitress brought his Zopie and Malathi asked for another cup of hot chocolate.

'I have to drive back,' she offered by way of explanation to his raised eyebrow.

The brief had no mention of specific disciplines. Pieter did not need to know, she had decided. Instead, the brief asked for names, ages, nationality, and field of study of each South Asian alumnus who had passed through the Dutch university system over the past twenty years.

'The data is public,' she said.

He nodded. 'I'll head to Utrecht Uni tomorrow.'

She shook her head. There had to be a go-between.

'They shouldn't know about us,' she added. 'The West Germans are also being considered for the programme by the Government of India, and they're quite strong when it comes to Engineering. I'd rather not risk the Germans or my own colleagues finding out and trying to scuttle my efforts.'

At the mention of the Germans, a familiar taste overpowered the Zopie that Pieter was savouring. It was metallic and memorial, and brought with it memories of his mother's smile. He flinched. The anamnesis of his mother waving at him and screaming at his father to take Pieter away was as fresh as if it had happened yesterday. An Ashkenazi married to a Protestant, she had been deported to Westbork that afternoon. He never saw her again. He had spent most of his adult life learning to keep nausea at bay, and it was still a work in progress.

Malathi gave him a thousand guilders.

'For expenses.'

He hesitated, then pocketed the brown notes. She downed the remaining hot chocolate and left. He ordered another Zopie.

Almost three weeks after they had interrogated Saha, on a cold and foggy first of December, the Duty Officer rang Arora at his home early in the morning. An IFS mandarin had summoned him to South Block post haste, he was told. At South Block, he was met by an Under Secretary of something-or-the-other, who verified his identity and had him sign an acknowledgement in triplicate before, finally, handing over the large package marked to him. Back at Main, Arora called Sablok and told him to report to work at once. In the thirty minutes that it took Sablok to reach Main, Arora had opened the package and inventoried its contents: there was a thick sheaf of photostats inside—typewritten records from seven Dutch universities—and telephone directories for every major Dutch city. After Sablok arrived, they went over everything Malathi had sent and decided on a standard methodology for analysing the data. The first step involved reading through each photostat to identify South Asians. Since the records didn't indicate nationality, they had to rely on names. Details of individuals with Hindu or Sikh names, as well as those with Muslim and Christian names of distinct South Asian origin were to be recorded in a master list. They began after an early lunch. By eleven that night, each one had worked through a few hundred pages.

'We're going to need to weed out Indians from our list, somehow,' Sablok said, rubbing his eyes. Arora was resting his head on the desk after his eyes had given up focusing on the typewritten text.

'The foreign office should have records of Indians who travelled to the Netherlands. I'll send for it tomorrow,' he replied.

Sablok groaned. More paper. It would take forever.

'Any possibility of Almeida giving us more pairs of eyes to go over all of this?' he asked.

Arora shook his head and returned to the stack piled before him. Almeida wouldn't authorise an extra paper clip till they showed some product.

By Wednesday, they had clawed their way through all the photostats and snagged a hundred and seven names between them. The foreign office had, after much prodding over Monday and Tuesday, sent a few hundred records of Indians who had studied in the Netherlands. After a cursory glance, Sablok noticed that the documents also contained details of people who had apparently travelled on business. Someone in South Block didn't like them much, he reasoned. All of Wednesday and Thursday, they cross-referenced their list of one hundred and seven names with the records sent by the Foreign Office which, in a display of fabled IFS sensitivity and helpfulness, were not sorted by year of emigration. Arora would read out a name from the list they had compiled, and Sablok would read through the emigration records to try and find a match. If the name was the same, they validated if the duration of study corresponded to the date of travel. Halfway through, Sablok had a crisis of confidence.

'What if the person travelled to another country—France, say—and moved from there to the Netherlands?'

Arora began to laugh. Over five days, the two of them had spent nearly ninety hours cooped up in that room, hunched over all the names in the universe. He was beginning to dislike the way Sablok shuffled in his seat every few minutes as if his bottom was covered with haemorrhoids. This aspect of the job depressed him and he caught himself wistfully recalling his years in the field. If Almeida could have somehow read his thoughts right then, he'd probably have laughed himself silly. There was no going back in the field, not after what had happened in Berlin in '65 when news of his son's death…He noticed Sablok giving him a funny look and realised that he was still laughing, had been laughing through the entire head trip. He excused himself to the bathroom at the end of the corridor, the least frequented one. It was empty. In its grimy mirror, he saw his cheeks glisten and hastened to wash away all traces of emotion. When he returned, Sablok had the good sense to act like nothing had happened, and they carried on with whittling down their list. On Friday morning, it contained twenty-one names. Using Saha's list of disciplines, they eliminated seven industrial engineers, four doctors, six civil engineers, and one architect. Of the three that remained, two were electrical engineers. The last one had studied metallurgy at Delft University. Two appeared in the Amsterdam telephone directory, the third one was from The Hague. Arora noted their particulars and prepared a brief for Almeida.

CHAPTER SEVEN

The Hague (the Netherlands)

Raheel Ahmad's luxuriant whiskers caught snowflakes and trapped them deep within their tangles as he raced from his modest home in Schilderswijk, a working-class neighbourhood in The Hague, to his car across the street, nearly tripping over his own briefcase in the process. It was still dark that morning, with an overcast sky packed full of clouds that promised more snow despite having blanketed the city overnight. The heat of the car melted the snowflakes by the time he had driven to the end of his street and was turning at the intersection. The trickle on his upper lip made him wipe at it and check the mirror for a nose bleed. The cursory inspection was interrupted by the sound of metal grinding on metal followed by a muffled clatter and a loud scream. His driver's side mirror was shattered. He pulled over and stepped out to the unnerving sound of a low moan from behind the car. A woman lay on the road next to the mangled mess that used to be her bicycle. In the dim light of morn, he saw her struggle to sit up and thanked his creator she was alive. A decade spent in Karachi as a Muhajir Ahmadi had left him with a deep-rooted mistrust of authority that bordered on fear. Eight years in Europe as an immigrant had made it worse. He was a God-fearing man, an economic migrant who feared standing out. He walked towards the woman, fighting the instinctive urge to get back into his car and drive away. Then he noticed that she was bleeding from her chin, large crimson drops staining the snow. He ran back to the car for something to staunch the flow of blood with, cursing himself for the momentary distraction that had caused the accident.

'Hey! Schapie, stop!' someone shouted, using a derogatory Dutch term for Turks. He turned to see a young Cloggy, clean-shaven of face and head, running towards him from across the street. Ahmad looked around; the street was deserted. He stopped moving towards the car, turned to the Cloggy, and raised his hands.

'First aid,' he shouted.

The Dutch man reached him and grabbed his arm tightly, then began dragging him in the direction of the woman. He towered over Ahmad and outweighed him by at least thirty kilos.

'This isn't Turkije. You can't run away,' he shouted.

The next few minutes were a blur of Ahmad protesting his innocence, the Cloggy alternatively admonishing him and being solicitous towards the woman, and the woman claiming she was alright. Then, after the shock began to wear off, she noticed the cuts, bruises, aches and pains. Her bicycle was a mangled heap of steel. The Cloggy said Ahmad's car had driven over it and insinuated that perhaps it had crushed the woman's leg too.

He let go of Ahmad's hand and helped the woman to her feet, muttering 'fucking immigrants' over and over. 'We should call the police,' he told her. 'File a complaint. Get him deported!'

Ahmad felt a familiar tremor. It had its roots in the anti-Ahmadi riots that had flared up in Pakistan earlier that year and brought with it the knowledge that he wasn't welcome back home either. He wasn't a Dutch citizen and his permit to reside and work in the Netherlands was in jeopardy. Standing meekly with his elbows pressed to his sides, he offered to pay the woman for her bicycle and for any medical care she might need. He shivered in the cold, but his shirt and undershirt were beginning to get soaked.

'No need to involve the police, really. She'll just end up having to fight the insurance company,' he said, retrieving his wallet and offering all the money in it to the woman. The Cloggy looked at the few hundred guilders and grunted. The woman was about to accept Ahmad's offer when he stopped her.

'You may have to take time off from work. It will cost you more than what he's offering. That's barely enough for a bicycle,' he said. 'And who knows where he might flee to after we let him go.'

'I'm not escaping anywhere!' Ahmad protested. Beads of sweat were now forming on his forehead. 'I work here in the Netherlands. This is all the money I have.' He showed them his now empty wallet.

The Cloggy clearly wasn't impressed and eyed the perspiring Pakistani with distaste. He ranted about how foreigners only pretended to work so they could receive benefits and wondered if Ahmad's so-called employers even existed. A few cars drove by, slowing down as they passed to take in the scene. Ahmad worried that a police patrol could drive by at any moment, effectively destroying the life he had carefully salvaged. Who knew what the woman might say to them? And the Cloggy would certainly present a vivid account of how he'd caught 'this Schapie fleeing from an accident.'

As much as he feared it, Ahmad found himself inviting them over to his house to pay her more money.

'We won't let you out of sight,' the Cloggy replied.

Ahmad helped the woman into the rear seat of his car. The Cloggy parked his large frame into the passenger seat. The bicycle remained where it had fallen. In the street opposite his house, the woman stayed in the car while he dashed inside to get money. The Cloggy got out and paced about. Ahmad had a thousand guilders at home. He brought back five hundred. The woman agreed that the amount was sufficient, then asked to use his bathroom to try and clean herself up. The Cloggy glowered at Ahmad until he agreed. He showed her in and the tall Dutchman followed, making himself comfortable in Ahmad's living room. He had a few bored questions for Ahmad which the latter answered distractedly, his attention focused on the closed bathroom door. When he explained that he worked in power systems engineering, the Cloggy perked up. He was a college student who hoped to study nuclear engineering, he claimed. Ahmad explained his job in detail, all the while glancing at the door and his watch in turn. The Dutchman was much friendlier now and asked if Ahmad ever worked with nuclear reactors. The immigrant shook his head; he designed transmission lines.

'Can I have your business card?' the Cloggy asked.

Quite brazen, Ahmad thought, considering the way he had behaved, but he was hardly in a position to decline.

The woman emerged, her washed face showing virtually no signs of injury. She continued to wince with each step, though. Ahmad was glad to see them leave, and rushed to work after a calming cup of tea, all the while grappling with the suspicion that he had been cheated.

Malathi sat at her desk with the papers in front of her. The last of the reports from the reconnaissance she had commissioned on the three men Arora had cabled her about had just come in. Raheel Ahmed. She looked at the other two reports. Qasim Sharif and Abdul Khan. A power systems engineer, a petroleum engineer, a metallurgist. As she prepared a cable, she hoped all this information would make more sense to Arora than it did to her, and that this whole exercise had not been a colossal waste of her time and resources.

Arora read the cable thrice. It had landed on his desk a little after 1 p.m. At 1:30 p.m., he marched into Almeida's office and demanded to be let in, clutching the cable tightly to his chest. The outraged assistant refused. He walked past her desk, knocked loudly, and stepped in.

'Sorry sir, this can't wait,' he told Almeida, matter-of-factly.

The matron charged in after him and threatened to drag him out by the ear. The incumbent waved her away, his narrowed eyes glued on Arora. She retreated after staring daggers at the intruder. Both men flinched as she slammed the door behind her.

'Such insubordination,' Arora muttered.

'Yes, there is a lot of that going around these days. Perhaps you should update your last will and testament. Now, what do you want?'

'We've found him!'

Almeida motioned for him to go on. Arora began to explain the methodology used, but Almeida cut him off.

'I know how you went about it. What have you found?'

'We had three suspects. The Resident just sent us their details. Number two works for URENCO, a nuclear fuel processing company,' Arora replied.

'Hurrah!' Almeida said, with not the slightest change in his tone or expression. 'What do you want me to do now that you think you

60

have him?' He had spent the morning butting heads with an Under-Secretary at the Foreign Office about the Resident in London who, it appeared, had ticked off the ambassador. He wasn't ready to share in Arora's triumphal cheer just yet.

'I want the suspect to be placed under round-the-clock surveillance, sir.'

'Are you quite sure this is our man?'

Arora nodded.

'Is he a nuclear scientist?'

'A metallurgist, sir.'

'So how does a metallurgist help Pakistan build the bomb?'

Arora hemmed and hawed.

'You haven't the faintest, have you?' Almeida remarked.

'I'm not an expert, boss. We can get you a technical brief if you want one, but you asked us to keep the expert away from this compound.'

Almeida wasn't too keen.

'Sir, at least let us find out from our expert how much damage this fellow at URENCO can inflict upon us. If it's trivial, I'll apologise and step away from the operation immediately,' Arora said testily.

'Do not dare threaten me,' came the sharp reply.

'It isn't a threat, sir. Call it a promise. We can't assess this person without the help of an expert.'

'Fine, bring him in. But before you do, I want a written brief explaining why this URENCO chap is who we think he is. And I want your expert to be debriefed in my presence. Until that happens, I will not authorise so much as a casual glance at the suspect.'

Arora quickly handed the page he was clutching to his boss. It was a two-paragraph brief.

Half an hour later, a bewildered Saha alighted from Sablok's motorcycle and, after security cleared him, accompanied Sablok to an empty room in the large office complex. Arora walked in a few minutes later carrying a copy of the cable with substantial portions redacted in thick, black ink.

'We have three suspects, doctor. Help us identify the troublemaker,' he said, handing the copy over to the physicist.

Saha read it carefully, fidgeting with his wristwatch all the while.

'This person—sorry, there's no name mentioned—he works for

Shell. I think that's a petroleum company, sir. You can rule him out.'

Arora nodded, having arrived at the same conclusion himself.

'The power engineer designs transmission networks. I don't think he would have any exposure to nuclear weapons. This metallurgist, he works for...URENCO, is it? What does URENCO do?'

Arora handed him the last pages that detailed each company's operations, information that was obtained from public sources. Saha read the two paragraphs dedicated to URENCO's business.

'They process nuclear fuel. So the most he could do is guide them in harvesting Plutonium from their Karachi reactor,' he said.

'Bingo!' Sablok cried out, exchanging a triumphant look with Arora.

'I'm sorry, this isn't extraordinary,' Saha said, dampening their spirits. 'The process to do that is well defined, and the French are even building them a Plutonium reprocessing plant. Besides, it still doesn't address their greatest challenges.'

Arora shook his head, annoyed at the speculation.

'Are you saying this URENCO fellow can't really help them?' he asked.

'Well, he can help—'

'Help meaningfully, doctor? Succeed where PAEC failed? Can he be their Oppenheimer?'

'I'm not sure.' Saha did not know what to say. He had been asked his opinion and he had given it truthfully. But there were limits to his knowledge and he wasn't comfortable speculating. Sablok saw Arora's face redden and stepped in.

'Doctor, would more information help you make up your mind?'

Saha clenched his jaw.

'This is absurd. The Pakistanis must have an ace up their sleeve,' Arora muttered in a low voice.

'I could ask my colleagues about URENCO. But I don't expect much,' Saha replied.

Arora slapped his fleshy palm on the table, making a disconcertingly loud noise.

'They obviously expect a lot from this Khan, given how much trouble they have gone through already. Do you think they fly PAEC scientists First Class to meet and greet nobodies?' The words were rushed and forceful.

'There has only been one meeting as far as we know, sir,' Sablok pointed out.

'Captain, I'll bet every worldly possession that they have performed a background check and completed the approach by now. And they wouldn't expose their chief nuclear engineer to this fellow unless he had something valuable to offer.' Turning his attention to Saha, Arora continued, 'Doctor, you keep going on and on about Plutonium. Isn't there another kind of bomb? Surely they aren't meeting this bastard in Amsterdam for fun.'

'Well...'

'Because if building a nuclear bomb based on plutonium was such an impossible task for Pakistan, wouldn't an intelligent person look at alternatives? And I don't see why we managed it, but they'll keep finding it impossible.'

'Can we make an international phone call?' Saha asked. He was blinking rapidly now.

'Yes, but none of this may be discussed on it,' Sablok replied. 'Whom do you wish to speak to?'

'Our representative at the IAEA might have details about URENCO.'

Arora bolted from the room and returned five minutes later. He grabbed Saha by the hand and took him to their office.

'The Resident will relay our questions to the representative and send the answers back to us. We'll do this over cable,' he said.

Handing Saha a pen and paper, he asked the physicist to write down his questions. Three minutes later the encoded cable was on its way to Vienna. The response arrived half an hour later. Saha's hands shook visibly as he read the cable: 'URENCO ENRICHES URANIUM IN THE NETHERLANDS AT ALMELO, NEAR AMSTERDAM.'

He took a deep breath. 'There are two broad types of nuclear weapons that work by fission. The first is the implosion type that uses Plutonium, the kind we detonated at Pokhran. These are difficult to build, although harvesting Plutonium isn't too complicated if you have a reprocessing plant—the kind the French are building. The other kind is called a gun type weapon. It uses enriched Uranium.' His breathing was rapid now. Pausing, he asked for a glass of water. Sablok poured one and he took a greedy gulp before continuing. 'The gun type is easy to build. Well, easy is a relative term here. It is simpler to build than an implosion type. But nobody has offered to build the Pakistanis a Uranium enrichment plant. And enriching Uranium is tough and extremely expensive. That was why I did not seriously consider it...' He stuttered to a halt.

'We broke their country in two, doctor,' Sablok said, grimly. 'I think it's safe to assume that money isn't their primary concern at the moment.'

'I am so sorry, I really am,' Saha blurted, his voice near breaking.

'Never mind the bloody apologies,' Arora butted in. 'Just how much damage can this man inflict on us? Can he help them enrich Uranium?'

'They will need a factory for that. The process is called gaseous diffusion. It uses a lot of electricity. Look, I'm not an expert. Some of my colleagues at BARC know a lot more—'

'We don't care for technical details at the moment,' Arora interrupted. 'We need to explain to our superiors that this Khan is dangerous. In your opinion, is he?'

Saha nodded, then weakly added: 'How can I help?'

'Let's go meet the boss.'

The next morning, Malathi received a cable instructing her to place Abdul Qadeer Khan under immediate surveillance. She was also directed to travel to Delhi at the earliest to meet Arora for a thorough briefing.

CHAPTER EIGHT

Sablok and Arora briefed Malathi at Main on a quiet Sunday. A large part of the day was spent explaining technical terms and what they suspected the Pakistanis of seeking from Khan. Arora had wanted to involve Saha too, but Almeida vetoed the idea. At 9 p.m., just as they were powering through a recap of Plutonium versus Uranium, the old man walked into the meeting room and sat quietly while the three spooks struggled with second-hand knowledge. He dismissed Sablok once it was over, but insisted that Arora and Malathi stay back for a short discussion on operational parameters. The young analyst slunk away through the graveyard of Main's ominously echoing corridors without as much as a word.

'You do not have absolute freedom,' Almeida said, his expression sombre. 'Arora is yet to prove to me, beyond the ambiguity of a faint winter shadow, that Abdul Khan can truly enable our charming neighbours to achieve parity. Until he does, with your help, of course, you may not materially impact the suspect.'

He was rather delicate, needlessly so in Arora's opinion.

'I don't have the assets to materially impact a suspect anyway, sir,' Malathi replied, weighing her words carefully as she studied the two men. One of them had recruited her from the IFS, and the other was her boss. 'But,' she added, 'should the situation warrant it, do I have your blessings to involve the Dutch security apparatus or, at the very least, anonymously point them in Khan's direction?'

A colicky infant on the flight to India had afforded her little more than two hours of sleep in miserly instalments, and that after forty hours of busy wakefulness at The Hague and Amsterdam. At 6 a.m. on Monday, she would have to report to the airport in Delhi to depart for Amsterdam. A briefing meant to take a few hours at best had stretched to consume the better part of a day, and she was yet to discuss logistics with the Case Officer. It wasn't the first time she had cursed herself for letting Arora talk her into giving up a promising career in the Foreign Service in favour of this profession of insomniacs.

'We can't direct the minutiae of an operation from HQ, sir,' Arora chimed in.

'I understand that quite well, thank you.'

Arora put his hands up and leant back in his chair.

'It has been such a long time, sir,' he continued, 'since either of us was in the field cursing the fat bastards at HQ for sending absurd instructions, or not sending instructions at all, that I had almost forgotten how counterproductive that can be and assumed you had, too.'

That drew a peal of laughter from Almeida, causing the imperial below his lower lip to jiggle. Malathi clasped her hands together and stared at a speck of dust on the table before her.

'It must be annoying to have to suffer two bickering old dogs,' Almeida said, addressing Malathi. 'I will leave the decision of involving the BVD to you. Do keep in mind that once we pull that trigger, the operation will, in a sense, cease to exist. Unless you are confident that there is no time to be lost, please consult me first. After all, when the excrement flies and lands all over, I will be the one summoned by celestial beings to justify each and every aspect of the operation.'

Malathi nodded.

'Our first priority,' Arora ventured, seizing a moment's silence to take the conversation in another direction, 'should be to gather evidence that Khan is acting on behalf of the government of Pakistan. At the same time, we need to understand the extent to which his efforts help their programme. If he is giving them peanuts in return for diamonds, we would be better served by not intervening; let them waste dollars. We also need to investigate the possibility of turning Khan to feed the Pakistanis dubious details, but that will come much later.'

The Resident and the Section Chief both accepted the broad prioritising.

'For the duration of this phase Captain Sablok and I will operate in shifts, ensuring that at least one of us is available here at Main at any hour of the day or night. A Teletext has been set up for our exclusive use. Here's the address and a set of One-Time Pads; I have the corresponding set in my safe. The machine will be continuously monitored.'

Malathi committed the address to her memory and, borrowing a Zippo from Arora, burned the scrap of paper on which it was scribbled.

'I do not wish to sound patronising,' Almeida began, 'but this being your first Tango with the Pakistanis, I feel compelled to warn you not to succumb to the party line: do not assume that they are buffoons, or that they are merely misguided but fundamentally like us. I've worked with them before partition and faced them as adversaries since. They are brutal, remorseless, and efficient. The amiable modernity is a facade. Expect no quarter.'

Malathi managed to look suitably sombre, acknowledging Almeida's concern with a 'Certainly, sir; I will; thank you.'

The old man then asked her for her assessment of the Dutch security establishment's attitude towards India.

'It used to be ambivalent, but after '71, sir, I wouldn't expect much charity unless Dutch self-interest coincides with ours. That's why gathering evidence of Khan's treachery against the Dutch state will be critical.'

'That will take time,' Arora added, pre-emptively.

Almeida smiled mirthlessly. 'That goes without saying. You have two months to show progress. Status every Thursday; monthly reviews by me,' he said to Arora.

'This is a strategic play for them, sir. Khan may not deviate from his daily routine even once in two months, leave alone incriminating himself,' Arora protested.

Malathi was happy to let Arora roll the operation up the bureaucratic slope, and held her tongue. Almeida looked at Arora without yielding so much as a twitch of an eyebrow.

'Come on, sir. Don't turn into an accountant at the peak of your career,' Arora pleaded.

'Two months. Monthly reviews.'

The voice over the phone sounded urgent: 'They have just taken a taxi to Schiphol. Three suitcases. All of them.'

It was six days since the briefing in Delhi; most of the Netherlands was going on vacation for Christmas. Malathi called someone she knew, a man with contacts within the airport. There was little time to waste, she told him. His instructions were clear: find out the Khan family's destination and report back before their flight takes off. She had commandeered the public telephone lines people dialled to enquire about visas to India. While each call went to the regular diplomatic staffer first, those callers that asked a specific question were transferred to her extension immediately. The sheer number of calls made on those lines would, she anticipated, mask the odd ones. Besides, the BVD were unlikely to tap a publicly listed embassy number; they didn't have the resources to analyse hundreds of random calls each day for each embassy and international institution at The Hague. An hour later, her agent called back.

'Can I apply for a visa that would allow me to travel to New Delhi from Karachi? My colleague Mr Khan will be visiting Karachi soon, and I hoped to spend a few days with him there before moving on to New Delhi.'

'That would needlessly complicate things,' she replied in the bored drawl of a public servant. 'Any application for a visa permitting entry from Karachi would be subject to greater scrutiny. Besides, I'm unaware of a suitable flight.'

'Oh, there is a PIA flight from Schiphol at 5 p.m. that flies to Karachi via a stopover in Istanbul.'

'I meant a flight from Karachi to New Delhi,' she lied. 'In any case, I recommend against it. Good day.'

She retrieved the One-Time Pads that Arora had given her. On a blank paper, she wrote: 'ABDUL KHAN EN ROUTE TO KARACHI VIA ISTANBUL. FLIGHT FROM SCHIPHOL AT 5 PM LOCAL TIME. ADVISE SURVEILLANCE AT KARACHI AIRPORT AND BEYOND.' Then she encoded it using the first

68

page of the One-Time Pad: she assigned a number for each letter on her message and each corresponding letter on the Pad, then added the two. The letter that corresponded to the sum became a part of the encrypted message. After feeding the encrypted message and Arora's teletext address to her machine, and receiving confirmation that the transmission had been received correctly, she tore the first page of the One-Time Pad and burned it along with the sheets she had written her message on.

It was 7 p.m. in New Delhi. Sablok had stepped out for a pack of smokes when Arora decoded and read the message. He rang Almeida's office and relayed the message, then made the request.

'I will make the call to Mishra,' Almeida replied. 'Let us see if Khan tips his hand in Karachi. Write up a formal request.'

Karachi (Pakistan)

The gossip columnist sat at a table next to floor-to-ceiling windows overlooking the tarmac, sipping her second cup of black coffee. It was 8 a.m. Karachi airport was slowly coming to life and, in a way, so was she. The previous evening had been busy: after a short stop at Qasre-e-Fatima, she had stayed at a party near CJM in Clifton till after midnight. The phone call at 5:30 a.m. on a Sunday morning had put her in a foul mood, but the coffee was slowly working its magic. Her photographer was outside on the balcony with a telephoto lens longer than her arm, waiting patiently for the flight from Amsterdam to land. He had received a tip-off that George Harrison was travelling to Pakistan for a personal, hush-hush tour of Sufi shrines.

'In disguise, of course,' he had added, 'and with a lady friend.'

'I'll be at the Sky Grill. Come get me when it's about to land,' she had replied before crawling into the restaurant under the crushing weight of a monstrous hangover.

Her editor had laughed when she had asked for a raise a few months earlier. 'Let's see him laugh later today,' she murmured to her cup of coffee, the warm china soothing the ache in her temples.

She was about to order a third cup when her photog rushed in and almost dragged her out. The flight was on descent.

'You go down to the tarmac. I'll get a better angle from here,' he told her. And so she rushed down the stairs and got as close to the aeroplane as she could. The excruciating whine of engines bored through her skull, reviving the headache the coffee had nearly drowned. She narrowed her eyes to tame the sunlight reflecting off the aircraft's windows. The ladder rolled up to the door. Passengers began filing down and walking past her to the terminal. Most were Pakistani: businessmen, the odd cricketer, students, families; there were a few firangs, but none of them resembled the Beatle. Fifteen minutes later, after all the passengers had left, the crew deplaned. She walked up to one of the stewardesses and introduced herself. Seeing a glimmer of recognition in the young woman's eyes, she warmed up to her at once. Could she please point out George Harrison from among the last of the passengers who were now almost at the terminal building? Who? George Harrison, the musician. Clueless. Very unattractive. The stewardess consulted the passenger manifest.

'He's British, isn't he?' she asked, scanning the list. 'No British passengers on today's flight, I'm afraid.'

'Could you check again, please?'

After another cursory look the stewardess confirmed that Mr Harrison wasn't embarking on a Sufi journey of the soul, and walked off to join her curious colleagues who were waiting a few yards beyond. She whispered something to them and the columnist heard laughter. Bitch!

Her photog was apologetic.

'Next time leave the investigative stuff to me,' she replied, narrow nostrils flared and delicate chin jutting out.

He took her back to the restaurant and ordered another cup of coffee to soothe her anger. She nursed her coffee mug, making a mental outline for a column about bitchy stewardesses.

'Later,' she told herself, paying no heed as the photog extracted the roll from his camera. She didn't notice him drop it into the ashtray at their table either.

New Delhi (India)

The cable arrived on Arora's desk at 2 p.m., half an hour before the photographs did. At 3 p.m., he rang Almeida's residence.

'You wanted hard evidence, sir,' he said.

70

It took the old man fourteen minutes to reach his office. Sablok handed three photos to him.

'Abdul Khan reached Karachi earlier today with his family. You can see him and his firang wife alighting in the first photo. He's the man with sad, wistful eyes. They were received by a uniformed man and two staff cars. The man can be seen shaking Khan's hand in the second photo. His name is Imtiaz Ahmed, a Lieutenant Colonel, one of Jilani Khan's boys. Mrs Khan and the children were driven in one staff car to Khan's family home in Karachi with all their luggage in the trunk. Lieutenant Colonel Ahmed drove with Khan to a hangar at the rear of the airport from where they hitched a ride in a PAF C-130 tactical transport aircraft,' he narrated.

'Islamabad?'

'That appears to be their destination, sir,' Arora chimed in. 'The cable hints at it.'

Almeida allowed himself a smile.

'Draft a suitable cable to Malathi,' he instructed. 'Then cable the Resident at Karachi and tell him to step away from the Khans. We do not want to spook them. Write up an appropriate report for the Secretary. And finally, gentlemen, congratulations. You have a real operation on your hands now. Do not cock it up.'

CHAPTER NINE

1975, Amsterdam & The Hague (the Netherlands)

Malathi began receiving detailed reports about the Khan household after an elderly Dutch couple from Rotterdam—Hendrika and Johannes de Wit—rented a house in Amestelle less than a hundred yards away from Khan's. They moved in quietly a week before Christmas Eve, on a weekday when it was snowing; those in the neighbourhood who weren't at work were huddled indoors around the fire. Barely anyone saw them. Even in the middle of winter, Hendrika couldn't help noticing the lovingly tended garden of number seventy-one, with well-pruned rose bushes and tulips that appeared ready to bloom at the first hint of spring. From the first-floor bedroom window of their house, the de Wits had a clear view of Khan's garden and front door. Taking care to remain in the shadows, one of them would always sit in a rocking chair a few feet back from that window, with a pair of binoculars close at hand. As December shed its skin and became January, their weekly reports documented the banality of the Khans' existence. The only redeeming feature Mr Khan could lay claim to, one of their reports said, was the intense competitiveness with which he played volleyball with his neighbours on the street on weekends. Khan, in Hendrika's opinion, seemed to be driven by an impulse to prove he deserved everything he was blessed with, and that impulse pervaded every aspect of his interaction with neighbours. Mrs Khan was a quiet and dignified lady, she relayed, a prematurely aged soul who derived meaning in caring for lost and broken beings. There didn't appear to be any significant strife in their marriage and, while the de Wits had avoided any contact with the Khans as instructed, they had no hesitation opining that the Khans' marriage was, for the most part, a happy one.

On weekday mornings, at 6:30 a.m., Abdul Khan drove his Ford Escort to the De Olm, Zwanenberg train station. From January, a taxi followed at a discreet distance. The passenger, a scruffy young man with an auburn goatee carved to look like Lenin's, followed Khan on his two-hour commute to Almelo. A college dropout who had flirted with anarcho-communism as a student, he had been recruited by one of Malathi's agents with the usual mix of money and ideology. He reported that Khan commuted alone, followed no fixed pattern, sat next to a new person each day, and was extremely chatty, sometimes painfully so. His Dutch was fluent and, although the dropout himself did not speak it, from the ease with which Khan conversed with a German tourist one day, it was evident he was comfortable speaking that language too. After a few weeks, the reports became terse. On one occasion the dropout, tiring of waking up early every morning, complained to his handler that the whole effort was a complete waste of time.

'He does nothing unusual at all, talks loudly enough to be heard outside the fucking train, and never sits next to the same person twice. There is no pattern.'

His handler gave him some extra money, convinced him of the critical importance of the work he was doing, massaged his ego, and asked him to continue for another month while he made alternate arrangements.

Hendrika and Johannes showed greater patience. Through January, each report maintained the same level of detail. They had begun to socialise with some of the other residents of Amestelle, people nearer their own age, and had learnt a good deal about 'that cute Dutch girl married to the Turk'. In the first week of February '75, in the midst of unusually cold weather, Johannes noticed a tall South Asian enter the Khan house late in the evening. Hendrika carefully dressed for the crisp breeze blowing outside, and went for a stroll. Despite the unwelcoming weather, the windows and curtains of Khan's living room were wide open, and she could see the top of the visitor's balding head. Soft strains of conversation in a foreign language taunted her declining hearing, but she couldn't understand a word. Anyway, it was too dangerous to stand outside their house for more than a few moments. There were three cars parked on the street that did not seem familiar; she noted the make and registration of each one. Walking to a public telephone a few streets over, she called their handler. The call connected to the practice of a moderately successful doctor on the other side of Amsterdam.

'Three unfamiliar cars,' she told the doctor after the call was transferred in by the receptionist. 'One of the number plates was foreign. Yellow letters on a green background. U 287 CD 27. It was a Volkswagen Passat. Do you want the local ones too?'

He did, so she told him, then hung up and returned home. Her husband was still at the window, his eyes glued to number seventy-one.

'You had me worried. I thought you were about to storm into that goat eater's house and demand to know who the other goat eater was,' Johannes quipped, his heavy jowls quivering as he chuckled.

Hendrika frowned. 'Someday you're going to call the wrong Turk that horrid name and suffer the consequences.'

'I knew Kastein and Wapperom! The focken mofs couldn't catch me,' Johannes began his usual rambling account, peppered with racial slurs for Germans, of the time they had both participated in the Dutch resistance as communists. Hendrika had heard the story hundreds of times, but, like always, she indulged him while he relived their only legacy.

The doctor had just finished seeing his last patient for the day when Malathi's call came. She had stopped at a public phone, detouring a few miles from her drive home. The doctor relayed reports about the Turk and the three unfamiliar cars. Malathi smiled when she heard about the unusual number plate. Green background and the letters CD indicated that it was a diplomatic plate of French origin; 287 meant that the car belonged to the Pakistan Embassy on Rue Lord Byron in Paris. After the call, she turned her car around and drove along a circuitous route, taking care to employ tradecraft. Once she

74

had assured herself that nobody was following her, she drove back to the embassy and cabled a brief account of the evening at Amestelle to Delhi.

'VISIT TO ISLAMABAD NOT A FLASH IN THE PAN,' was how she chose to end the message.

Three minutes later, a reply came through: 'ADVISE WAITING FOR A SECOND VISIT; MIGHT BE A COURTESY CALL.'

The shrill ring of the telephone intruded into Arora's pleasant dream. He was still half in it as Sablok read out Malathi's message, sounding like a child who had just received a pet puppy. Arora asked him to repeat the message, a little slower this time. It sank in on the second attempt.

'One communist does not a politburo make, Captain,' Arora replied, his voice hoarse and sleepy. 'Ask her to do nothing until there is another such visit. It might be one of the diplomatic staff sent to gently let Khan down. Thank you for your interest, but unfortunately, we are unable to make use of your apocalyptic skills at the moment. We'll keep in touch. Something like that.'

'Aren't you being a bit too cautious, sir?'

'They wouldn't use a vehicle with diplomatic plates so brazenly. Too great a risk of exposure. Let's wait and see.'

Sablok had hoped that this breakthrough would mellow Almeida's demeanour towards him further, even though the events at Karachi had softened it considerably already. He was a dhobi ka kutta, serving two masters—Almeida and Mishra—and rightly guessed that neither fully trusted him. It was a hole he had dug for himself, and it was up to him to climb out of it. But Arora was the Case Officer. If he wanted to wait, then they would wait. Acutely aware of his own lack of experience when it came to such an operation, he encoded the message to Malathi and transmitted it.

The cable she transmitted the next morning was verbose, detailing everything the de Wits had reported including the fact that the visitor had stayed until midnight.

'Perhaps they insisted that he stay for dinner,' Arora said, only half believing his own explanation. It was too late to do anything about it anyway. Sablok had other ideas.

75

'Within a Pakistani embassy's hierarchy, where do the Residents fit in?' he asked, leaning forward, his eyebrows raised.

'It depends on the ambassador, to be honest. But they're usually posing as mid-level diplomats, just like ours.'

'No, I meant where do they fit into the unofficial hierarchy? How much pull do they have?'

'Quite a bit,' Arora replied. 'Most of them come from the Pakistan Army officer corps. Those chaps are very tribal when it comes to defending one of their own. If a Foreign Office chap crosses swords with a Thug, nine times out of ten the thug will win.'

Sablok lapsed into silence. Then he drafted a cable to the Resident in Paris and handed it over to Arora for review. It relayed the diplomatic number plate and asked the Resident to determine if the Volkswagen Passat was in the Pakistan embassy's shared pool. If it was used exclusively by an individual, the Resident was to provide as much information about him or her as he could.

'I saw a few of their officers up close in '71 before open hostilities commenced. Unbelievably self-entitled. If an ordinary officer could be like that, I imagine a bright one in the ISI would very likely be lording it over everyone else,' Sablok clarified. 'The vehicle is a new model, I looked it up. It is the kind that an influential member of an organisation may reserve for his own use.'

Arora looked at him, his unkempt eyebrows raised in question.

'You're making a lot of assumptions,' he said, finally, 'and generalising about their officer corps. They're not all that different from us, Captain.'

Sablok shrugged. 'My experiences with them have been different then. Anyway, this won't cost us anything,' he said, pointing to the draft cable.

Arora shrugged, mimicking the younger man, then asked him to transmit it.

The Resident replied two days later: The car wasn't in the embassy's shared pool; it was used by Tahir Hussain, Third Secretary. The cable ended with the Resident's suspicion that Mr Hussain was his Pakistani counterpart.

Arora wrote to Malathi asking if she could arrange to capture audio from Khan's house. She replied that she had neither the equipment nor the expertise to carry out such a task. Arora went to Almeida

76

with the request for a technical team to facilitate gathering audio from Abdul Khan's living room. There was none available; the lion's share of any resource in the Wing went to the Pakistan section.

'Not that I grudge Mishra the shiny electronics he monopolises. The Cabinet Secretary really leans on him in the quarterly reviews,' Almeida added.

'Perhaps if you requested Section Chief Mishra to lend us—'

'Not without a credible and imminent threat. Besides, we have no technicians in our section capable of setting it up and operating it. It takes four adults to move that vacuum tube monstrosity of a receiver. Using that thing in Amsterdam will be a logistical nightmare. We don't have the means to sneak it past customs, so it has to travel in a diplomatic bag. But then it will end up at the embassy in The Hague. How do you move something weighing a few hundred kilos from there to Amsterdam without the BVD sniffing it out?'

'Could it be set up in a van or a truck?' It was a shot in the dark.

Almeida laughed.

'I'm sorry, Jugs. Make do with what you already have.'

'That should be easy, sir; we don't have anything,' Arora replied, with a wide grin.

'In my day, we didn't even have that luxury,' Almeida replied.

Arora walked away, shaking his head and muttering about James Bond never having to deal with this kind of stuff.

A viscous week went by, then three. Reports about the mundane domestic life of Abdul Khan continued to come in, as did trite accounts of his commute to Almelo. With each passing day, Malathi's fear that the visit was nothing more than a courtesy call, as Arora had predicted, grew. The argument was reasonable. And yet the person described in the reports, who had offered to commit treason against his adopted country and had gone the extra mile to do so, showed no signs of being rejected. The idea of spying for your country was gut-wrenching enough even with the safety provided by the Vienna Convention. The decision to do so without those protections took huge moral commitment, which was why, in her experience, ideologues made better spies. People who had invested a substantial portion of their soul in a cause often crumbled when the cause did not want them anymore, and it showed in their behaviour. Khan's nonchalance despite the ISI supposedly rebuffing his overtures was extraordinary, and that raised the possibility that he hadn't been rejected at all.

Like most evenings, she was at her desk contemplating this anomaly and ways to dig deeper, when her phone rang. It was her direct line, a number she seldom gave out. The caller, a middle-aged lady with a voice that reeked of a few packs of smokes every day, wanted to inform Mrs Singh that her appointment had been moved to the next week as the doctor was unavailable that Saturday. Malathi answered that although she wasn't Mrs Singh, she would convey the message. Minutes after the call she transmitted a coded message to Delhi. It was Arora's turn to sleep next to the Teletext that night, and he was in the middle of a dream involving Marlene Dietrich when the machine whirred to life and chased Ms Dietrich away. He decoded the message almost mechanically, the result of more years spent using One-Time Pads than driving, but the words took time to sink into his glamour-addled mind. When they did, the smile that Ms Dietrich had left him with broadened into a grin: 'ANOTHER VISIT BY THE PAKISTANI; DIPLOMATIC PLATES.'

Over the years, Malathi had oriented her networks towards multilateral agencies, a natural resource with which the Netherlands was truly blessed and, as a consequence, her ability to sustain and expand surveillance of a target was acutely limited. With the section unable to provide electronic capabilities, it fell upon Arora to plug the holes in the dyke. It was upon his insistence that the forty-three-year-old German photographer, an agent of his from Berlin in the '50s, was read into the operation. He landed at Schiphol late in the afternoon and was waved through customs when he showed them his West German passport. Till eight in the evening, he killed time at the Arrivals lounge, reading most of Doctor Faustus and consuming most of the café's stock of coffee. A taxi then took him to Halfweg-Zwanenberg, where he went through one and a half rolls of film photographing commuters at the railway station. When a policeman noticed him and walked over, Mark neatly recruited him to the cause of his visual essay on the less touristy side of Amsterdam, and shot a few images of the cop sheepishly leaning against a lamp post, his navy blue peaked cap resting at a rakish angle on his head. Mark had with him a portfolio of photo essays from the streets of Brussels, Berlin, and Bonn, and regaled the policeman with anecdotes for fifteen minutes while the latter pretended to appreciate the artistic values of dark, grainy photos of average-looking people.

After the policeman had adjusted his cap thrice, wished him pleasant shooting and walked away, Mark headed south across the canal and then west, camera in hand, looking for whatever it was that street photographers sought. A film roll later, he found himself in a quiet residential neighbourhood made of clusters of one-storey houses with extensive gardens. Walking along the streets and lanes of Amestelle, he came to house number seventy-one. The shutter sounded deafeningly loud when he stood far back in another house's shadows and expended an entire roll taking pictures of seventy-one, bringing back unpleasant memories of Mosin-Nagants. It was a cold night and windows were shut tight. Nobody noticed him. Walking to another house further along, he replaced the 35mm with a longer lens and took close ups of each of the visible windows. The living room of seventy-one was empty but the lights were on and he was able to take enough shots of the interiors to deduce the layout of the room. Satisfied that he had covered every available angle, he crossed the street, turned his back to seventy-one, and took photos of houses that faced Khan's. Then, after wasting another few rolls on a leisurely walk around the cluster, he rang the doorbell of the house at the end of seventy-one's lane. It was a little after 11 p.m. Johannes had just finished a nap and was getting ready for a long night of keeping watch on Abdul Khan's house when Hendrika answered the door and welcomed Mark. She showed him to his room, which was already equipped with everything he needed for developing photographs. He would stay as her nephew for the next few months.

At 8 p.m. on the seventh of March, the black Passat with French diplomatic plates stopped outside seventy-one. The balding, tall Pakistani stepped out and walked slowly and calmly to Khan's doorstep. He was apparently expected because Khan opened the door before the visitor could reach for the doorbell. They hugged each other warmly—old friends meeting in a foreign land—and went inside. Mark had taken sixteen photos of the visitor and his car by the time the door to seventy-one closed, five of them clearly showing a face with an aquiline nose and light eyes. He then wound the film roll and handed it over to Hendrika, went downstairs to the kitchen, and helped himself to two bottles of beer. Over the next two hours, as residents turned in to sleep and the windows in the lane began to go dark, he slowly sipped from one bottle and spilt from the other onto his clothes. By 10 p.m., after two more bottles had soaked his cardigan and shirt, he smelt like a brewery. Lights in the Khan living room were on and the windows open, absurd given how cold it was. The rest of the house appeared deep in slumber.

Mark detached the M3 from its tripod and, separating the long lens from the body, placed both in either trouser pocket. Slipping out of the house, he walked to a streetlight opposite seventy-one and sat quietly near it, his eyes darting from one house to another. When he felt that nobody was staring out of any window at the madman out in the cold, he pulled out a small pair of insulated pliers from his shirt pocket and ripped the wire feeding the streetlight to pieces, making it appear to be the work of an angry canine. The portion of the street outside seventy-one plunged into darkness. In the silent dark, his ears strained to hear the sound of a window or door being opened—some reaction to the lamp suddenly going out. Nobody cared. The only sound came from a door at the end of the lane and Johannes appeared soon after, ostensibly on a walk, but ready to create a distraction should Mark need it. After he was at the end of the path, he turned and glanced at Mark. Taking his cue, Mark swiftly moved a few steps back until he found himself next to the front left wheel of a car parked outside a closed garage door, then hoisted himself onto its bonnet and waited for an alarm to sound. Crouching for effect, he then launched himself at the roof of the garage, a flat surface a few feet above him. Pulling with all his strength, Mark scrambled over the edge and lay still. The garage was attached to a house whose bedroom window, shut against the cold air, was a few feet to his left. When the lights of the house did not switch on, he allowed himself to breathe a bit easier, then turned around so that he was now facing seventy-one.

Thirty feet away sat two men, their backs to him. The curtains were open, and they seemed engrossed in some documents; two diligent colleagues burning the midnight oil—nothing out of the ordinary. Except that in this case, they happened to be committing treason. Mark retrieved the camera and lens from his pockets and put them together. Feeling a dent in the lens body, he panicked and cursed himself for carrying the equipment so casually. Peering through the viewfinder, he took the lens through its full zoom range. The glass appeared intact, and so was his plan. Aiming at the open living room window, he zoomed in on the documents that Khan was reading from, focused till the eleven-point font was clear, and began clicking. Each shutter release was like a cannon shot. He had to fight the urge to look around after each photo to make sure he wasn't exposed even though he knew Hendrika and Johannes were watching his back from either end of the lane. The sound of a beer bottle being smashed on the road would be his warning. For the better part of an hour, he lay still on the garage roof and clicked photo after photo of technical documents, blueprints, and handwritten notes.

He was winding exposed film from his sixth roll of the evening when the bedroom light to his right came on and, almost simultaneously he heard a glass bottle break in the street below. Mark lay still, his attention divided between seventy-one before him and the window to his right. Khan's guest poked his head out and studied his car for a few moments before glancing up and down the street. Mark could hear his own heart beat louder than the camera shutter had sounded, and wondered what Johannes was prepared to do if the guest spotted Mark and decided to confront the strange man taking photographs from the top of a garage. Smashing a bottle and slamming a door was easy enough, but would the old man pick a fight with a spy to save another? Look away, go back inside, fuck off, he willed. And yet the guest remained at the window. It was then that Mark noticed the window to his own right was no longer lit. He heard footsteps, then a door opened and closed. The guest was staring in his direction now. Only a matter of time. Mark shrank into the roof and lowered the lens slowly. Run, the primal part of his brain screamed. Shuffle back! He will see you! But his years in Berlin with Arora returned to him. The guest was looking out at the dark night from a brightly lit room. He wouldn't see much, but he might sense movement.

Footsteps sounded, too close for comfort, and too heavy to be the old man's. A car door unlocked and opened, suspension creaked, the door slammed shut. Khan's guest was staring right at him. Mark lowered his head just before the car he had used to get to the roof started, its headlights illuminating the garage door. As it reversed into the lane and turned, Mark kept his head down, his eyes closed. The lens was pointing at the garage roof and would not reflect the car's light; neither would his eyes. He stayed that way for an eternity, then slowly, ever so slowly raised his head. The guest was now back inside Khan's house and the door was closed, the two men back to reading the documents. Mark detached the lens and stowed it and the body in his pockets, moved forward till he was at the very edge, then slowly lowered his body until his feet were about a metre above the ground. He jumped, landing as silently as he could on the balls of his feet. His knees would hate him for a few days. Turning casually, he strode from the house, away from seventy-one, just another resident out for a midnight smoke.

CHAPTER TEN

'Phone call,' the night attendant slurred. Reddish drool descended from a corner of his mouth and his hair was a greasy mess. Saha had been reading a monograph and couldn't hide his irritation at the interruption.

'Who is it?' he snapped.

'Don't know,' the attendant replied, his bleary eyes rolling upwards in protest.

'He must have given a name,' Saha insisted.

'Some Captain-shaptain,' came the reply.

The guilt that had taken weeks to abate returned in an instant and a panicked Saha hurried to the reception desk of the guest house.

His breath came out in sharp, heavy bursts as he spoke into the telephone receiver: 'Hello, hello. Saha speaking. Hello?'

'Doctor Saha, good evening. This is Captain Sablok…'

'Yes, Captain. Very good evening. Saha here. Is everything okay?'

'All good so far, sir. I'm on my way to your guest house. Is fifteen minutes sufficient?'

'Sufficient?'

'Yes. We need to go to the office. It's urgent.'

Saha's stomach churned. His sense of responsibility conflicted with a deep sense of dread and it left his mind in an effervescent state of confusion. He still felt ashamed about having neglected to take the possibility of a gun-type weapon seriously, and had hoped he would never have to face the spooks again, especially the obese one whose resigned disappointment had reminded him of his grandfather. Waiting for Sablok's arrival, Saha paced the length of Guest House's lobby .

Forty-five minutes later, he was at Main, struggling with the blurry writing on two dozen photos. He rubbed his eyes and blinked violently, straining to read. The photos were marginally out of focus and telegraphic transmission had not helped any. Saha's right knee bounced with metronomic precision. Going back and forth among the photos in the warm light of an ornate table lamp, he searched in vain for clear text as Arora's pudgy fingers hammered a dirge on a corner of the table.

'Would a transcript help, doctor?' Sablok asked, throwing a lifeline to the visibly flustered physicist.

'They were prepared by laymen,' Arora cautioned, his tone curt. The fingers continued without pause. 'They will be very inaccurate. Better if the doctor draws conclusions from the originals for himself instead of relying on someone else's interpretation. The blueprints may help.'

The last few photos, which had been held back till then, were diagrams for a machine of some sort. Saha turned his attention to them, making out two concentric cylinders with a bearing of some kind between them. The inner cylinder was only supported by the bearing; he deduced that it was meant to rotate. It was a guessing game. He was unfamiliar with the machinery involved; physicists had little to do with engineering, especially theoretical physicists like him. Nothing he had seen throughout his education or his work at BARC could approximate, in his stressed mind, to the drawings before him. His first instinct was to assume that they were fuel rods, but the shape was wrong. Besides, fuel rods did not need to rotate. He had suggested to Sablok, the last time he was called in, that they consult with engineers at BARC. Evidently, that piece of advice had been ignored.

Saha was keenly aware of his own limitations but felt the intense pressure to give them something useful, to compensate for past mistakes with brilliant insight. The presence of Sablok and Arora's boss in the room only made matters worse. He persevered with the blueprints for a while, then returned to the documents. A word caught his eye; it was blurred, but he could have sworn it said CENTRIFUGE. Something inside his mind clicked into place. He asked Sablok to check if the transcripts contained references to centrifuges; after shuffling through the transcripts a few times, Sablok replied in the affirmative. Weak with relief, Saha reached across the table, took the transcripts from Sablok, and began reading their typewritten text. It was a gas centrifuge made of Maraging steel, with three openings to the rotor: one to input gas, and two to collect the different factions. Arora had informed him at the beginning that the product was from URENCO, so Saha guessed that the gas would be Uranium Hexafluoride or HEX. The two factions would be two different isotopes of Uranium.

This was absurd! Uranium isotopes were nearly equal in mass. The speed at which the centrifuge would have to spin to meaningfully separate them would be phenomenal. Almeida noticed Saha's expression flit from the joy of discovery to something nearing futility.

'Speak up, man,' he commanded. 'What is it?'

Saha told them.

'Can the Pakistanis use it to—what was the term?'

'Enrich Uranium, sir,' Sablok answered.

'Yes, to enrich Uranium. Can they use this contraption to do that?' Almeida asked, his tone sharp. It had been a long day filled with more than its share of the usual bureaucratic vacillation, and he had grown weary of ambiguous responses.

'Well...Theoretically, they can, sir,' Saha answered.

'Theoretically, Arora here could burst into flames and solve our energy crisis,' Almeida replied, an unmistakable edge to his voice. 'And would you please stop pretending to be Alla Rakha for a few minutes?' he snapped at Arora, who stopped drumming immediately and pulled his hands back to his side.

Saha tried to explain that the two isotopes were very similar in mass. The closer two components of a gas or liquid were to each other, in terms of mass, the faster they needed to be spun to separate them. Any centrifuge attempting to separate two isotopes of Uranium would need to spin unimaginably quickly.

'And yet some creative soul did imagine it, did he not?' Almeida retorted.

Saha had no data, but they expected him to give them an authoritative answer. Ordinarily, he would have refused. But this was no ordinary situation, and these were no ordinary men. So he did the next best thing his traumatised mind could think of and clammed up. Almeida sighed and shook his head. Arora had assumed an expression of existential disappointment at the very beginning of the meeting, and it remained in place.

'Doctor,' Sablok said, his tone soothing, 'We are not worried about the theoretical.' His words were meant to be kind; his expression, conciliatory. 'More than anything else, our objective here is to determine if the information being sold to the Pakistanis is genuine. Will it help them along the path to developing the bomb? And if it does, how much of a difference will it make? How expensive will it be? We need to calibrate our response and the answer to this question is an important part of that—'

'Allow me to cut to Hecuba, Captain,' Almeida interrupted. 'As Minister of Foreign Affairs in 1965, Bhutto swore that if India went nuclear, the Pakistanis would eat grass if they had to, but they would get a bomb of their own. Now, if this fellow in Amsterdam is swindling dear old Zulfikar by selling him technology that does not work, I am happy to step aside and let Bhutto eat grass till Resurrection day.' A smile crept over Almeida's face as he said that. 'But when you say that theoretically a centrifuge can enrich Uranium, it makes us all nervous. Is this one of those "theoretically possible, but practically impossible" things that humanity may grapple with centuries from now? Or will Bhutto have enriched Uranium within the next decade?'

Saha exhaled. When he spoke, his voice was a monotone. 'With all due respect, sir, fuel enrichment is a vast field of study in its own right. I don't possess the expertise to—'

'Fine. Who does?'

Saha suggested a colleague from BARC, a senior scientist. Almeida relayed his particulars to an underling over the phone and asked to be connected without identification.

'Obviously, doctor, the three of us here in this room do not exist for your colleague. Nor does this organisation. Please do us the favour of getting the answers we need from him.'

'At this hour?' Saha cried out, shaking his head. 'It's past midnight. He is quite senior to me. How do I justify the urgency?'

'Blame the Cabinet Secretary, doctor. It is what I always do,' Almeida remarked, unable to hide a hint of glee. 'Tell your colleague that the glorious leader of India's steel frame has demanded a briefing from you. First thing, of course. Nobody questions the urgency of a task when you take the Lord's name.'

Saha giggled despite himself and Sablok smiled politely. Almeida saw that Arora was still looking glum, almost suicidal.

'Oh, wipe that scowl off your face, Jugs. It makes you look like Sartre and Camus had a love child.'

Arora's expression worsened; Almeida laughed. The phone rang a minute later. Arora handed it to Saha. The colleague, a mild-mannered man of forty, sounded groggy. When Saha explained the reason for the call, making sure to drop the Cabinet Secretary's name thrice between many apologies, his colleague audibly perked up and seemed eager to help. Saha could hear his colleague's wife murmur in the background, but that stopped after a few moments of complete silence during which the colleague had presumably retreated to the privacy of his study.

'Can a gas centrifuge be used to enrich Uranium?' Saha asked when he came back on the line.

'Yes, theoretically.'

Almeida, who was listening in on another handset, grimaced when he heard that adverb.

'Has anyone managed to operationalise the method? Even if it's experimental, I'd like to know,' Saha said.

There was an extended pause. Saha waited, then began to suspect that the line had gone dead. He was about to tap the cradle when his colleague spoke, mentioning a German engineer at the University of Virginia who claimed, in a paper published years earlier, to have developed centrifuges that enriched Uranium for the Soviets.

'I was a doctoral candidate back then. My guide and I had a few discussions about that paper, I remember. We never heard more from that person. I guess he was silenced.'

'How credible did your guide find it?'

'Very. It's just an engineering problem, really. Spin it fast enough, and you can separate the isotopes. The challenge lies in getting the right material for the rotor because weaker metals can disintegrate at ninety thousand revolutions per minute.'

Saha asked if he remembered the journal and the name of the author. His colleague did not, but promised to find out. Saha thanked him, apologised once more, and rang off.

'The Pakistanis are not being duped, sir. They have a viable path to enrichment,' Saha told Almeida once the handsets were back on their cradles.

'Are you certain of that?'

'The problem has to do with structural strength. The outer edge of a rotor just twenty centimetres in diameter, when spun at ninety thousand revolutions per minute, travels at twice the speed of sound, give or take. The material has to be robust enough to withstand the forces acting on it. If they had the process working in the '50s, as my colleague confirmed, then they certainly have it working very well by now,' Saha answered.

'I think we ought to consider the fact that the solution to this materials problem is being provided to the Pakistanis by a metallurgist. That cannot be a coincidence,' Arora observed.

'Right. We proceed with the understanding that the product being promised to the Pakistanis is genuine. It is a shame, really. I was hoping to nominate that metallurgist for a Padma Shri for conning Bhutto,' Almeida quipped. 'Doctor, I know it is really late, and I hate doing this to you, but would you be so kind as to write your thoughts down for us? Here, use this pad. Arora, give him your pen, please,' he added, shielding the Montblanc Meisterstück clipped to his shirt pocket with the palm of his hand. 'And do endorse it when you are done. The bureaucrats that we report to are physiologically incapable of reading an unsigned document, I am afraid.'

Amsterdam (the Netherlands)

Khan's handler had begun visiting him every week. The change in tempo suggested that they were now dealing with larger volumes of information. Mark repeated the exercise of climbing the garage to photograph them once more but was almost caught when the person who owned that house woke up and looked out of his bedroom

88

window. Mark escaped by jumping off the garage into garden towards the rear of the house, and then scaling the fence to run off into the large open area behind the house. The de Wits later assured Mark that neither Khan nor his handler had noticed, and Mark was prepared to give it another go the next time around. After reading the report the next day, though, Malathi instructed that such risks did not need to be taken anymore, and that was that. It was better, from an operational perspective, for Khan to continue meeting his handler at home. They were sloppy and Malathi wanted them to remain that way.

A week later, the watchers noticed the presence of a Dutch man at the meeting. He was young and seemed awkward, but he stayed on for dinner. The handler engaged him in lively conversation and the sound of laughter could be heard from the house through the evening. The man left at 10 p.m. and was seen off by Khan at the door. Mark decided to follow him to find out where he lived. The party that had raged till then died abruptly and, fifteen minutes later, when Hendrika strolled past seventy-one, she could see Khan and his handler engrossed in reading documents. The next morning she visited the doctor once again, passing on a report on the events of the previous evening. It included photos of the Dutch man and an address: an apartment block on the outskirts of Almelo that housed six families. By observing which apartment's lights turned on a few minutes after the man entered the building, Mark had worked out that he lived in apartment five. The nameplate said he was Frits Veerman. A day later, Mark was able to confirm that Veerman too worked for URENCO. He was a shy introvert who loved photography, and worked at the Almelo facility as a machinist.

The next few weeks saw Veerman visit Khan almost every other day for dinner. On more than one occasion, Khan's handler was around to engage him in casual conversation. Khan always waited for Veerman to leave before retrieving documents and discussing them with his handler, though, and, as far as the watchers could tell, Veerman was not carrying any documents to or from the house. Malathi's assessment was that Khan and his handler were attempting to recruit Veerman, but had not been successful yet. New Delhi concurred. She decided to recruit him herself. That would give her a source capable of reporting on Khan's conversations with his handler and, based on

Khan's requests to Veerman, she would be able to identify the extent of Khan's knowledge. Arora was doubtful but had the grace to assure her that he would back her up regardless of what happened. Almeida was far more sanguine, so the decision was made.

Mark travelled to and from Almelo a few times with his M3 and a 50mm prime lens in full view. As he had hoped, he saw Veerman ogling the equipment. A smile and a wave later, he was seated next to the young Dutchman while the latter gingerly handled Mark's camera. For an hour, as the train travelled from Almelo to Schiphol, they talked about photography. Veerman was an enthusiastic amateur, the unofficial staff photographer at his workplace, who took all the photos at staff picnics and events. He was impressed by the professional who claimed to be doing a street photography project in the main cities of Europe. Mark promised to show him his portfolio the next time he was in Almelo, and Veerman gave Mark his home address and telephone number. Alighting at Schiphol, Mark waited half an hour at the train station before travelling to Zwanenburg.

A few more days went by before Mark rang Veerman up one evening and dropped in with a fat stack of photographs. From then on they met almost every week, often spending whole weekends taking photographs of people on the streets. Mark insisted on supplying the film.

'I have benefactors,' he told Veerman.

Communication was mostly in slow English: Mark spoke poor Dutch, and Veerman's German ended at Eins-Zwei-Polizei. Veerman was fascinated: here was someone living the life that Veerman wanted for himself. It was the sort of meeting that seemed predestined. Mark laughed when Veerman self-consciously rued that it would take him decades to hone his skill to a point where he could do what Mark could.

'You have good eye, Frits,' Mark assured him. 'Someday I'll introduce you to my benefactors. They will like the photos you take.'

Sometime in the middle of May, the watchers noted Veerman's arrival at seventy-one and settled in for a long night. An hour went by without Khan's handler showing up. Then they saw Veerman leave. He seemed agitated, walking with quick and short steps, arms crossed across the chest, hands tucked into the armpits. Mark noticed through the binoculars that his face was ashen and decided this was the opportunity they were waiting for. He instructed the de Wits to use the emergency contact procedure and ran after Veerman. Khan must have botched the recruitment; there was no other explanation. It was imperative that he get on the same train as the distraught young man. A hard sprint at Halfweg-Zwanenburg ensured that he boarded the same train a few bogies behind Veerman, and he moved to a few seats behind him when they changed trains at Amsterdam Centraal. He was worried Veerman would notice him prematurely, but the young Dutchman was in his own personal purgatory, staring far into the distance without actually seeing anything. That gave Mark time to check his own tail. He couldn't spot anyone and, assuming there was no tail, settled down to plan his approach. It had been many years since he had tried something like this, and Mark was worried he had become rusty. His instructions had been clear: the Resident would make her way to Almelo independently and meet them at Veerman's apartment as soon as Mark gave her the signal. That gave him a few hours to make his move. He decided to do it at Apeldoorn, two stations before Almelo.

The number Hendrika dialled rang in Malathi's office. The old lady gently asked to speak with Mrs De Jong and was brusquely told that no such person lived there. She persevered, asking if this was the De Jong residence at twenty-seven, Handelstraat, and was told emphatically that it was not. The line went dead. Malathi gathered a briefcase, stuffed a fat manila envelope from her safe into it, and told the Duty Officer to drive her to the railway station. It would take her longer to get to Almelo than it would Mark and Veerman, leaving her little margin for error. She barely made it on the last train of the evening for Almelo.

Mark had left his camera at the de Wit's home, and it gave him the perfect excuse. Shortly after the train left Apeldoorn, he walked towards the front of the bogie and sat on a vacant seat just ahead of Veerman. Head resting on his hands, Mark emoted weariness and loss with the felicity of a thespian. A few moments later, to drive the point home, he let out a low wail: 'Nein! Nein! Nein!' People glanced at him, one or two passengers asking if everything was alright.

'Mein camera was stolen,' Mark replied, his voice loud and hoarse. More heads turned to look at him. Veerman recognised the voice even before he laid eyes on his friend. Mark made a big show of relief when Veerman tapped him on the shoulder and sat down next to him, gripping his hand tightly. He even managed to shiver a little, distressing the already distraught Veerman even further.

'Mein camera, my money, passport. Gone. A thief. Ran away with the bag. Very precious. M3. Four lenses. Documents. Gone,' he babbled over and over.

'You complain to police?'

Mark shook his head but continued babbling before Veerman could ask any more questions. At long last, he allowed himself to be calmed down and they travelled the rest of the way mostly in silence, each man stewing in his own misery. At Almelo, Mark stood aimlessly on the platform after getting down from the train. Veerman asked what he was going to do.

'I don't know,' Mark replied, staring at the horizon. He looked utterly helpless, a far cry from the dashing photographer who normally exuded such confidence. Veerman took pity on him. He insisted that Mark join him for drinks, and began walking towards the exit. Mark did not budge. Finally, Veerman hooked an arm into his and led him out. It was just after 10 p.m.

Almelo (the Netherlands)

Malathi's train pulled into Almelo Station at 10:45 p.m. She hailed a taxi and directed it along a circuitous route to a neighbourhood near Veerman's, annoying the driver by acting confused and making him drive around in circles a few times. There, she checked into a hotel that a Third Secretary at the Embassy had once recommended, a modest three-star suitable for an austere civil servant from a third-world country. Her dash from the embassy had been indiscreet, but the need to recruit Veerman outweighed the risk of piquing the BVD's curiosity. She hadn't noticed a tail, either on the train or during the drive afterwards; a competent surveillance operation at such short notice, unless she was already being followed by a team of watchers, could safely be ruled out.

Inside the room, she switched off all lights after a few minutes, then carefully peeked from behind the curtains: this was a small city and traffic had already died down, but a considerable population of drunks was milling about; a couple leant against a street lamp for support and took turns retching. Almelo had been a major textile centre after the war, but fierce competition from cheaper producers had bankrupted the industry and left thousands unemployed in the late '60s; the city was rife with resentment against foreigners. For the first time in years, Malathi felt the need to close her eyes, take a deep breath and will herself to do what she had to. She inventoried the contents of her briefcase in the light of a table lamp, slipping a switchblade knife into her trouser pocket in anticipation of a fifteen-minute walk to Veerman's apartment. Then she waited by the phone.

Beer was too mild an anaesthetic for grappling with their demons, so Mark and Veerman began downing whisky to take the edge off. Veerman was solicitous and commiserated about Mark's camera and lenses. The thought that someone would rob a photographer wandering around on unfamiliar streets with a small fortune in equipment had really shaken him up. It wasn't artifice; Veerman's concern seemed genuine. He was a kind soul, Mark decided; socially inept, but completely without malice. He hated what he knew he would have to do to Veerman that day. It would crush the young man, make him question his own judgement.

'Push them into purgatory, then shine a torch on the only path to heaven,' was how the process had once been described to him.

Sometime between the third and fifth peg of whisky, Mark managed to reverse roles and become the solicitous friend, asking after Veerman's disturbed state of mind and gently prying information out of him. By eleven-thirty, they were ready to leave. Veerman had opened up and was lamenting about a friend of his who was asking him to steal from their employer. Mark had the opening he needed. Instead of diving in, he bid Veerman good night and asked, in a rather embarrassed tone, if he could borrow some money for a cheap hotel room.

'My friend here tomorrow with money for me. I will repay,' he added.

Veerman was concerned about letting him wander off on his own. Confiding in him had made Veerman feel a bit better, and he wanted to unload further. He insisted that Mark could sleep on his couch that night, and refused to take no for an answer. Mark protested, but not too much.

Veerman's apartment could only be described as frugal. The interiors were bare and seemed to be exactly as he had found them when he moved in. A clean but worn-out couch and a tall lampshade made up the furniture of the living room. Although there was enough space for a television or record player, there was none. The only defining feature was a print of Ansel Adams's Moonrise, Hernandez, New Mexico—a stark photo of the moon taken at twilight. Its presence was at odds with every other aspect of the apartment and Mark guessed that it wasn't something that had come with the house, a relic of a prior occupant; Veerman had brought it with him and obviously treasured it. He stood before it quite deliberately, a supplicant at the altar, until Veerman noticed and began speaking about it. As they communed over the works of Adams, Veerman brewed coffee in the open kitchen. They talked about Monolith, expressed reverential awe about The Tetons and The Snake River, worshipped Church, and raptured at the thought of the photos of the Taos Indian woman dressed in white and carrying an earthen pot over her head. Coffee had blunted the excesses of whisky by then, and Mark deftly let the conversation segue from Adams's photographs of Japanese-Americans interned during World War Two at Manzanar, to how some nations oppressed their own people.

'It must have took courage to show Japanese-Americans kindly when das government demonised them,' he murmured, adding, 'Don't you agree, Frits?'

Veerman nodded. He had become quiet and thoughtful as Mark continued to pontificate, throwing heavy sentiment at a young man struggling with right and wrong to deliberately overwhelm his moral compass.

'My own parents and their generation. My father was a Nazi, ja, a low-level functionary in an small, rural Kreise of the party. Mother later said he was not an evil man. I believe her, sometimes. But good men closed their eyes and ears while their government murdered millions. He died when the Soviets invaded. Mother and I survived, somehow.' Mark's grey eyes hardened. 'We feel good these days, ja? Nazis are history. Mass murder is in the past. What is it called? The English have a word for it.'

'Genocide,' Veerman offered. His voice was heavy.

'So antiseptic, ja? Genocide. We feel bad when we hear of millions killed. Then, we feel smug. It cannot happen again, we tell ourselves.'

Mark lapsed into silence, eyes staring at the wall before him.

'We have learnt from the mistakes of the past,' Veerman finally said when the silence became uncomfortable.

'We have? Do you think all the evil people are dead? You're too young. Those of us born before the war…Have you ever met a Nazi, Frits?'

Veerman shook his head.

'I have. He is an old man now. Do you know what his unit did? They caught a Russian woman in the East. She was searching for food, he told me, because her child was hungry. The city was under siege and there was no food left: all the dogs had been eaten, their bones gnawed of gristle. She was looking for rats. Someone said she was a spy. Everyone knew she wasn't, but it didn't matter. She was just a Slav, they reasoned. They dragged her into the truck and took turns beating her breasts with the butts of their rifles. Then they had her, one by one. Eight men, Frits. When they were done, they threw her out of the truck and, as she lay there writhing in agony, they threw grenades at her. She didn't scream anymore, the old man said.'

Veerman looked ill. His mind was overwhelmed, and he didn't notice that Mark's fluency in English had suddenly undergone a marked improvement.

'Another man, one of my neighbours back in Deutschland,' Mark continued after giving Veerman a few minutes to digest it all. 'Very polite man. Goes to church every day, loves his wife, dotes on his children. I got him nice and drunk once. He was in the Wehrmacht, he told me. His unit was there during the Polish occupation. He told me he still remembered shooting people. He liked going for women, especially women with prams or those walking with children. Seeing their blood splatter on their child gave him a thrill he still remembers. But shooting children was very difficult, he told me.'

Veerman's face told Mark it was only a matter of time.

'He said, "The bloody children moved too much to shoot them properly,"' Mark continued. 'This evil—these are our fathers, our uncles, our brothers, and our friends. This genocide isn't even in the past, Frits. I went to an exhibition earlier this year in Berlin. There were photographs taken in Bangladesh. Do you know about Bangladesh? Good. One photograph in particular remains stuck in my head. I have tried to erase it with alcohol, but no amount of whisky helps, Frits. It was a photograph of a dog chewing on the thigh of a child—maybe five years old, maybe less. The child had starved—you could see his ribs—but someone had also stabbed him in the bloated stomach. You know how, when children starve for days and days, their stomachs become bloated? His intestines were hanging out. Do you know what the worst part was, Frits? The child was still alive.'

That was the final straw: Veerman bolted for the bathroom. Mark heard him expel coffee, whisky, beer and the sandwiches they had eaten earlier. When he returned, shaken and almost out of his mind, Mark looked him in the eye and asked: 'How much did the Pakistanis offer to pay you to help them murder civilians, Frits?'

CHAPTER ELEVEN

A little before 3 a.m., minutes after the night manager at the front desk was rudely shaken from slumber by a phone call seeking 'Miss Mal, who checked in late last night' and had grudgingly connected the caller through, Malathi checked out. She paid cash at the front desk and enquired about a taxi: there were none available, the night manager told her, advising her against leaving before dawn. She thanked him for his concern, but said it was imperative that she leave and, in the absence of safe transport, she would walk. The night manager watched her step out onto the street, turn right, and walk out of view. He worried about her for a while and thought of calling the police, but decided against inviting trouble and drifted off to sleep, his head resting on the front desk, dreams of the Bosphorus calming his soul.

Malathi's footsteps rang out on cobblestones like gunshots and echoed off the houses that lined either side of the street. She took to walking on the tarmac, which muffled the crack of her cowboy heels a bit. Her strides were long and quick, poised to break into a run, and she looked over her shoulder often, her eyes wary and watchful. There was little need for her to employ the finer aspects of tradecraft to disguise her heightened state of alertness; a lone woman walking down any street at 3 a.m. was hardly expected to be unworried, and vigilance was healthy. There was, of course, the abnormality of her walking out of a hotel with a briefcase at an unearthly hour, but that could not be helped.

On that desolate road, Malathi remembered the time she had stayed out past the 5 p.m. curfew during college days, only to be thrashed and abused by her aunt. The absurdity of the memory brought on a sharp, painful gust of mirth and dulled the edge of her anxiety. The noise startled a drunk sprawled beyond a parked car, or perhaps he had been lying in wait. He shouted at her, his slurred words mostly meaningless. Glass shattered a few yards behind her, an inadequate, empty bottle bearing the brunt of his frustrations. Malathi hugged the briefcase to her chest and ran. No more staying inconspicuous, no more avoiding routes that the police patrolled. Her breath became a deafening rasp after a few hundred yards, and the pounding of her feet sounded like three people in pursuit. Snot clogged her nostrils and oozed down her upper lip, her tongue dried up and stuck to the inside of her cheek. Legs ached, then burned. Seared lungs made each breath an ordeal as they fought to suck in more air. Sweat streamed down from her jet-black hair and pooled in her brows before stinging her eyes, impersonating tears and then breeding them . She couldn't have been more than a mile from Veerman's house when training overcame adrenaline, and she slowed down. Deep, deliberate gulps of air eased the thumping in her chest. She lowered the briefcase and held it by her side, listening carefully for aberrations; the night was silent as death itself. Instead of continuing along the street to Veerman's apartment, she turned into an alley, cradled the knife with her right hand, and hoped that the path did not lead to a cul-de-sac. She zigged and zagged along alleyways, often circling back and standing still in dark doorways for minutes at a time, always looking for moving shadows and listening for footsteps, for the sound of a car, for the growl of a dog. Her fear was firmly on a leash. After thoroughly satisfying herself that she had not been followed, Malathi finally entered Veerman's apartment building and softly knocked on the door to his apartment.

Veerman and Mark were both bewildered by the sight of the diminutive, dark-skinned woman dressed in black trousers and a blue blouse stained dark by sweat. She was armed with nothing more than a briefcase against Almelo during witching hour, and had obviously walked a long way to stand in Veerman's doorway.

'Please wait outside,' she said to Mark, who quickly recovered from the surprise and stepped out, pulling the door closed behind him. The soft click of the latch sounded deafening at that hour. He sat in the stairwell, the canary in the coalmine. He had deliberately preyed on the emotions of a naive young fool suffering a crisis of conscience, and a part of him had enjoyed it like it always did. The poor fellow had been so distraught and drunk that he hadn't protested Mark's accusation even once or denied that Khan had tried to recruit him. At one point Veerman had lashed out at Mark's betrayal of their friendship, but it had been trivially easy to deflect it to Khan's greater deception before Veerman's anger hardened. Mark felt like gloating over how deftly he had used Veerman's own sense of outrage, and loathed himself for feeling that way. The last time he had softened a prospective like this had been a decade ago. Like then, he felt nauseous. Feeling his pockets for a pack of smokes, he deeply regretted giving up the habit a few weeks earlier. He considered knocking on the door and bumming one off Veerman or the Resident, but settled instead for an old mint that he found in his trouser pocket. It tasted of detergent.

'I am not asking you to betray your country or URENCO, Mr Veerman. As a matter of fact, I am here to help you to stop betraying it. May I sit?'

When Mark had told Veerman that he was calling a colleague over, the young Dutchman, a nervous wreck by then, had expected a sadistic German or two, the kind who played SS Sergeants in World War Two movies. The woman sitting on his sofa hardly fit the bill. Before Veerman could recover , Malathi handed him a black-and-white photograph of a naked, half-eaten corpse lying on the road beside a rice field. He glanced at it, then recoiled, his eyes darting away. She sat quietly and made no move to accept it back from his desperate, outstretched hand.

'Do them the courtesy of looking,' she said after a few moments. The cold fury in her voice drew his attention back to the photo in his hand. She could see what little colour had remained drain from his face. She knew how he felt. She had desensitised herself to their horror by forcing herself to go through the photographs over and over in the privacy of her office, away from intruding eyes that might see her reaction. She had known that she could not afford to flinch if she was to use them to recruit Veerman. Even so, sitting in his living room, she had to breathe deep to keep her partly digested dinner down.

'These were victims of the Pakistan government, innocents murdered because of their ethnicity.'

The next two photos she gave him were of a similarly distasteful theme: one showed corpses lying face down in a waterlogged field, their hands still tied behind their backs; the other was of a man kneeling at the edge of a pit full of bodies, staring hauntingly at the camera as a soldier prepared to shoot him in the head.

'That's the last Jew of Vinnitsa,' Malathi said, pointing at the kneeling man. 'I'm sure you recognise the soldier's uniform. They killed six million, many of them your countrymen: Jews, Gypsies, homosexuals, artists, intellectuals, and anyone else whose face or beliefs were, to them, distasteful. It took them four years—from '41 to '44. This other picture,' she indicated the first picture, 'was taken four years ago in what was then East Pakistan. The Pakistan government and their army, for whom your dear friend Abdul Khan works, murdered three million: Hindus, Muslims, homosexuals, artists, teachers, students, doctors, intellectuals, off-duty soldiers, and policemen. It took them just eight months, two weeks, and three days.'

A photo of a four-year-old child, dead, a crow plucking at its remaining eyeball, made Veerman retch, though there was nothing left in his stomach to expel.

'They did not feel the need to spare children,' she said.

Veerman was transfixed, his gaze bound to the child's half-eaten face and the crow's busy beak. Malathi closed her eyes, took a deep breath, then removed the next one from her briefcase and pushed it into his hand. Veerman registered her discomfort at a subconscious level.

'They raped four hundred thousand women after their religious leaders had proclaimed that women in East Pakistan were legitimate war booty for Pakistani soldiers, many of whom Abdul Khan counts among his close friends.'

The photo showed a disembowelled woman from one side. Her hands were tied to a lamppost behind her, and she was hunched forward at an angle that suggested that her shoulder had been dislocated. Not a scrap of clothing covered her decaying flesh. Intestines lay scattered outside the body and her head, twisted in the direction of the camera, held a grim smile on it, her eyes staring straight into the viewer's soul.

'Girls as young as eight were abducted from their homes, imprisoned in special camps, and repeatedly raped by those soldiers.'

The horrific realisation that the subject of the photograph he held in his hand wasn't a woman but a little child filled Veerman with visible revulsion and horror. Malathi steeled herself and looked at the photo. This particular image had disturbed her for hours when she had first seen it. It had even infiltrated her dreams.

'Many of them,' she began speaking, before choking on the words. 'Many of them committed suicide by hanging themselves from the ceiling, using their own hair for a noose. Imagine the desperation that drove them to do that, Mr Veerman. Then imagine the barbaric cruelty of the Pakistani soldiers, who responded by cutting every living captive's hair off, denying them their only route of escape. Such is the company your friend keeps.'

By then Veerman was sobbing. His entire body was in the grip of involuntary spasms. The next picture brought out a wail.

'Once they were done raping women, they often bayoneted their genitals and left them to bleed to death. Look at the photo, Mr Veerman. Look! This is the reality that Abdul Khan's friends cloak behind their suave modernity and barbeque parties.'

She held up another photograph, a more recent one taken at Amestelle.

'Recognise this man? Let me refresh your memory. You had dinner with him at Khan's house. Here's a photo of him in the uniform he wore for twenty years: Colonel Ejaz Khan of the Pakistan Army, currently on deputation to their intelligence agency. As a Lieutenant Colonel in command of a regiment, he personally murdered seventeen students at the University of Dhaka. He also kept a personal harem of six abducted women and children for five months. Did you enjoy the barbeque lamb you ate with him? Was the meat tender and moist? How was the conversation? Did he advise you on the finer aspects of bayoneting a vagina, Mr Veerman?'

She did not have hopes of using him to spy on Khan anymore. He was a complete wreck. If his nerves somehow held, which she doubted,

Khan was unlikely to trust him again. And even if Khan did display incredible naïveté, his handler surely wouldn't. Veerman's eyes had blanked out, expressing nothing at all. She gently tapped his hand. He recoiled from the sudden contact, but she could see his mind return to the present. She showed him one final photograph.

'If you confront Khan, he will claim innocence. "Of course I don't know about Ejaz's real profession," he will say. "I had no idea that he was a spy. Or an officer in the army. I swear, Frits, I know no army officers." When he does that, you will think me a liar. So here he is, your friend, at Karachi airport last Christmas. The man shaking his hand is Lieutenant Colonel Imtiaz Ahmed, once again of the Pakistan Army, once again a soldier on deputation to their intelligence agency. Ahmed flew your friend on a Pakistan Air Force jet to Islamabad to meet the Prime Minister. I'm told they spoke for hours. But obviously this is very normal and any engineer visiting Pakistan on vacation gets an appointment to meet the PM. Ask your dear friend to set you up. The PM may wine and dine you too, and Ejaz may—'

'He is not my dear friend!' Veerman roared, his eyes flashing rage. Malathi calmly waited for him to continue, but guilt had dulled the outrage already, and he had run out of things to say. At the moment, the only thing he knew for certain was that Abdul Khan was not his friend.

'Frankly, Mr Veerman, I couldn't care less. Don't feel sorry for yourself. These are intelligent, evil people trying to use you to further their goal of killing millions more. But you can redeem yourself. You have that opportunity. Take it. I promised you that you wouldn't have to betray your nation. I am not concerned with the secrets themselves, just the questions Khan has been asking you and the requests he has made. Can you help me with that much? Are you looking for redemption?'

Veerman nodded after a few moments of thought, a feeble motion of a broken person. Malathi discreetly activated a tape recorder inside her briefcase and began the debrief. It was first light at Almelo.

Malathi reached the embassy at 3 p.m., retrieved a One-Time Pad from her safe and a bottle of Scotch from her desk drawer, filled a cut-glass tumbler almost to the brim, and began the arduous task of transcribing the debrief and then encoding it. With a little probing, Veerman had succumbed to the urge to confess everything to her, starting from the time he had first noticed Khan's strange behaviour nearly six months earlier, but had attributed it to the challenges faced by any immigrant in integrating into an unfamiliar society. Halfway through it, she had let Mark go, instructing him to step up surveillance at Amestelle: if the Pakistanis got spooked by Veerman's hostile reaction, she needed to know immediately. Then she had returned to wringing Veerman dry.

Transcription took four hours; encrypting it took another two. A third of her bottle was empty by the time she had transmitted a detailed report. Going home for rest was out of the question. She locked herself inside the office and surrendered herself to a few nightmare-ridden hours of sleep as Saturday bled into Sunday.

The shrill ring of the bedside telephone at 5 a.m. snapped Almeida out of whatever it was that higher bureaucrats dreamt of, and the voice at the other end of the line coaxed him to drive to Main half an hour later. Instead of heading to his own office, he stepped off the lift onto the second floor and walked in on Arora and Sablok laughing like teenagers at what had presumably been a dirty joke.

'You were a man of God once, sir,' Arora said, refusing to share the joke. Sablok giggled quietly.

'Two months at the seminary doesn't make someone a man of God!' the old man protested.

Arora opened his mouth to speak, then shook his head while holding his own earlobes. The old man gave up and sat on the chair Sablok had vacated for him.

Sablok summarised the long debrief that they had received.

'It appears they have moved on from concerning themselves with the design of these centrifuges to the logistics of procuring the components required to build them,' he ended.

Over the next hour, he and Arora walked Almeida through each sentence of the report, highlighting parts that indicated the extent to which the Pakistanis had progressed. The old man was suitably alarmed.

'I want one of you to type me a memo summarising the operation. The other one will work with Malathi to prepare a list of options for stopping Khan. Make sure you consult her on the capabilities of her networks to act on each option, as well as her assessment of the most likely outcomes. Be pessimistic. Both documents will travel up the chain of command, so make sure they're precise. I will meet the boss tomorrow morning. Have them ready by tonight. And for heaven's sake, tell me the bloody joke!'

They did.

CHAPTER TWELVE

Malathi awoke abruptly. The noise of hundreds of letters being hammered onto paper by the manic spirit of her Teletext filled her office. A hangover had wrapped its tentacles around her head, soaking her in self-loathing. The faint flavour of stale Scotch mingled with the stench of two days spent without brushing teeth and worsened the post-adrenaline blues she had delayed with alcohol. At 4 a.m. on a Sunday, the embassy was a graveyard, with only the Duty Officer in the communications room in the basement as the keeper of this extremity of the Indian republic. She downed a spoonful of salt and two glasses of water. The brine came back up, bringing with it the acrid contents of her stomach. She washed up as best as she could, then returned to her office and decoded the message. It spoke of three courses of action to deal with Khan, asked her to assess her network's capability to execute each one, as well as the anticipated outcome: they could eliminate Khan, hand over incriminating evidence to the BVD, or get the Dutch press involved to force the government's hand. She had considered these scenarios many times since Khan's perfidy was first established with the photograph at Karachi airport, and the answers came quickly.

A discreet number of doors away from the PM's own office, in a cul-de-sac that few even knew of, was an office marked "Research". Almeida sat inside, his dark brown leather briefcase straddled between his legs, and waited for the Secretary to read through the memo. It took that remarkable man, responsible for making the Wing what it was, less than five minutes. In a soothing, gentle voice that belied the shadowy power he wielded on behalf of an oblivious Republic, he began with a compliment. 'This is excellent work,' he said. 'To go from a cable about air tickets to nuclear proliferation in Europe in a matter of months!'

Almeida allowed himself a smile in acknowledgement, then got on with business: 'We have worked out three scenarios, sir, and would like authorisation to initiate number one.'

His boss glanced through the last two pages of the memo once again.

'Are you confident that the information—these design details—have not reached Pakistan already?' he asked.

'Documents have not been removed from Khan's house by his handlers since December last year,' Almeida replied with practised tact.

The Secretary looked up from the memo and, staring at Almeida over the rims of his spectacles, gave him a moment to clarify. When Almeida did not, he spoke:

'One need hardly carry physical documents in the age of subminiature cameras; you know.'

Almeida nodded in grudging agreement. The inability to penetrate Khan's house rankled.

'It cannot be helped, I suppose,' the Secretary continued. 'Assume the worst case: every document has been photographed and studied in Islamabad. In such a scenario, how does killing this Abdul Khan retard Pakistan's desperate scramble towards parity?'

Almeida took a few moments to compose an answer.

'We consulted a scientist from BARC who had worked on our own Peaceful Nuclear Explosive, sir.' That drew a rare smile from his boss. 'It was his opinion—and our secondary research supports it—that Pakistan's challenge lies in engineering the device, not in designing it. They lack the know-how and the manufacturing facilities to enrich Uranium. Their quickest path to a working nuclear weapon is to import all the equipment. Since no manufacturer will sell them an assembled centrifuge—indeed, there are none that we know of—they must purchase individual components and assemble them on their own. This is where Khan becomes critical to their plans. He knows, or can find out, details of suppliers of those components across Europe. In fact, just last week, Khan tried to recruit a Dutch colleague and sought precisely those details from him. That tells us the Pakistanis don't have every piece of the puzzle yet and Khan is their only conduit. There is also the possibility that Khan has already established a network within URENCO. Eliminating him might sever it from his handlers for good.'

His boss nodded in a leisurely manner.

'Do we plan to involve the Dutch? It says here,' the Secretary said, reading from the memo, 'the Resident has established contacts within Amsterdam's criminal underbelly, the Penose.'

'Yes, sir; she has.'

'Presumably, we would use their services to eliminate Khan?'

Almeida nodded in reply. He was about to elaborate on it when his boss spoke once more.

'That leaves us exposed to the possibility of being detected. After all, the memo indicates that these contacts have been recently forged and, as a result, remain untested. We have no means of evaluating the Penose's competence. If the criminal fails, Khan will almost certainly be extracted by his handlers; the ISI will not believe, even for a moment, that an attempt on their agent's life was coincidental. And that isn't even the worst outcome. What if it turns out that her contact works for the Dutch police or even the BVD? As an organisation responsible for internal security, they're certain to have infiltrated criminal groups; the Bureau has.'

'Those possibilities cannot be dismissed, sir. In the absence of a stated policy on liquidating...shall we say, "irritants" the Resident must accept these operational risks. About the BVD, our Resident firmly believes their response won't be to our liking.'

'Is she saying that Dutch counter-intelligence would not be interested in unearthing a mole?' The tone was one of incredulity.

'In a way, sir, she is saying just that. And I would like to add that I have been unable to poke holes in her rationale. Two factors work against us: '71 and the Soviet veto has made NATO suspicious of us, and any intelligence we give the Dutch against Pakistan—a member of CENTO and SEATO—may find itself being whispered to the Pakistanis themselves; then there is the inconvenient fact that any prospective employee of URENCO has to be vetted and cleared by the BVD first. If we hand this over to them, we will actually be accusing the BVD of incompetence—not exactly something that will inspire an aggressive investigation. They may even attempt to brush all of it under the carpet. Viewed within the context of the brazen openness with which Khan meets his handlers, it does not engender confidence in the BVD's capabilities or motives.'

'I see here that she doesn't favour using the Dutch press either.'

'She reasons, sir, that the BVD stepped up infiltration of newspapers after the student protests of '69, and any story we leak to the press can, and likely will, be squashed before it makes a difference.'

'How far do you trust her judgement, Almeida?'

'Far enough, sir.'

After a few minutes of idle chit-chat, the Secretary stood to indicate that the meeting was over, and thanked Almeida for the briefing.

'Given that the option for eliminating Khan carries with it the risk of our Resident getting embroiled, we must get the diplomats' blessings. We wouldn't want them to unilaterally withdraw her diplomatic protections, whether out of spite or for containing the fallout, when she needs them the most. If I may indulge in some plain-speaking, the domestic political climate is already having an impact on our foreign relations and, unless the situation changes radically, I fear that blessing may not materialise.'

The Khans had enjoyed street volleyball and barbeque with a few neighbours on Saturday and had spent Sunday morning tending to their roses and tulips. There was no apparent panic at seventy-one, which led Malathi to believe that Veerman, against all expectations, had disguised the revulsion he felt at Khan's attempt to recruit him. Hearing nothing from New Delhi by Monday afternoon, she visited Veerman's apartment in the evening, timing her arrival within a few minutes of his return from work. He invited her inside and offered her a cup of coffee. The living room had been scrubbed clean, its meagre furniture rearranged; Moonrise no longer hung from the wall, leaving in its place a faint outline of dust and a bare nail.

She began by asking if he had been to work, hoping to get him talking again as he had on Saturday. This time his answers were curt, and he volunteered very little beyond what her question asked. There were no digressions. Wary of the change in his behaviour, Malathi gingerly broached the topic of Khan's actions, attempting, as she did so, to kindle Veerman's moral outrage and bait him into an emotional surge that she could then harness. But he remained distant and calm. Thrice she tried, thrice he batted her efforts away, taking long pauses between sentences. Tiring of walking on tiptoes, she asked if he had changed his mind about making sure Khan and his handler paid for their crimes. Veerman smiled. His eyes remained blank.

'I haven't. But I'm not going to run to you just because he scared me. I phoned my manager from a payphone today to warn him about Khan.'

She smiled and continued sipping coffee. This was a setback, of course, but the advanced stage of the operation mitigated its negative impact; New Delhi was already considering having Khan killed.

'You made the right choice,' she told him, setting the empty cup down on the floor by her feet. 'Please don't openly speak out against him. His handler is a brutal man. If you find yourself in a tight spot and need help, call this number and tell them your name. They'll know what to do.'

The business card had only a telephone number printed on it. She asked him to memorise it and return the card to her, which he did. Malathi left without so much as a goodbye.

Tuesday went by without a word from New Delhi. Malathi had never been involved in an operation that needed the elimination of an enemy agent, so she ascribed the delay to procedure. Counting on a green light from above, she began to lay the groundwork by activating the part of her network that had recruited a mid-level operator in Amsterdam's criminal underworld, a drug lord's enforcer. Unlike Friday evening, she exercised extreme caution, using every bit of tradecraft that she had learnt and mastered over the years to maintain deniability. There were two cutouts—individuals with little knowledge of the bigger picture who, if caught, would delay the investigators from finding out about Malathi long enough for her to make counter arrangements—between her and the enforcer, and the message they relayed—nothing written, of course—was innocuous to them but alerted the enforcer that someone needed to be murdered in as banal a manner as possible. Details would follow. Till then, he would finalise on one or two candidates to do the deed, known junkies who would have no hesitation in doing the job in return for a quick fix and the promise of more to follow. It was Wednesday afternoon when a chalk mark on a particular window told her that her message had been received. Inside her office, Malathi counted two thousand dollars and put them in a shopping bag inside her safe. Anticipating the possibility that the enforcer or the junkie may turn out to be a police informant, she drew up detailed plans for the first cutout to disappear abroad for a few months immediately after the murder was green-lighted. If there were an investigation, his disappearance would slow it down, allowing her to tie up loose ends and return to India before her involvement was discovered. All that remained for her to do was wait.

On Wednesday evening, right about the time Malathi was wrapping up preparations four thousand miles away, Almeida paid a visit to South Block and waited for the Secretary to emerge from a meeting with the PM's Private Secretary. He had called ahead for an appointment, but had been informed that urgent matters had led to the boss clearing his schedule for the rest of the day. Furious, he stormed into his boss's office and demanded that they send a note into the meeting to inform the Secretary that Section Chief Almeida was waiting in his office to hear about the decision. In reply, he received an apology: the Secretary regretted that he was unable to meet him right then.

'I am pressing the case, but there are other, greater concerns occupying everyone's minds at the moment. Tomorrow should bring with it some much-needed clarity.'

On his way out of the office, Almeida saw the Director of the Bureau hurry into the Private Secretary's office. He looked worried. So the concerns were domestic, Almeida reasoned. For a moment, he considered making discreet enquiries, but decided, instead, to mind his own business for once and stay out of politics. Rather than return to Main, he drove to Golf Links for a quiet drink and an early dinner, leaving well before the usual gaggle of Secretaries and Additional Secretaries descended upon the club to pat themselves on the back for "maintaining the nation despite the politicians".

Arora had stalked Almeida since Wednesday morning; he wanted an answer. Each passing day of delay carried with it the possibility of the surveillance on seventy-one being discovered. If Khan or his handler noticed it, they would slip out of Malathi's grasp. If the BVD chanced upon the de Wits and Deutsch Mark, as Arora had often called him back in Berlin, not only would they lose Khan and his handlers, but also run the risk of the BVD trying to roll up Malathi's networks. Every second wasted in moral justifications and political calculus risked the lives and well-being of the agents involved. When Almeida didn't return from his meeting on Wednesday evening, Arora decided to intercept him the next morning. He reached Main at 5 a.m. and parked himself outside his Section Chief's office. Almeida's assistant arrived at eight but merely raised an eyebrow at him and said nothing. Almeida arrived at nine, later than usual, and motioned Arora to follow him in.

'A decision has not been taken yet, but it appears that they are inclined to wash their hands of this entire episode, dumping it all into the BVD's lap,' he said the moment the door closed behind Arora. 'And before you begin propounding whatever arguments you have cleverly thought up, or start implementing some hare-brained scheme to force my hand, let me save you the trouble: I am in full agreement with Malathi's recommendations. Khan needs to be eliminated. Immediately. Unfortunately, that is not my cross to bear.'

Pushed off balance by the unexpected candour, Arora took a few moments to collect his thoughts.

'Surely, then, it is just a matter of scaring the leadership into approving what needs to be done, sir.'

'Must you be so artless? Do you think I painted a heavenly picture of brotherly love and peace for the Secretary, or he for those who must decide? I would be very surprised if his warnings did not invoke within them the odour of brimstone. The leadership is terrified, Jugs. Just not of the things we want them to fear. Any moment now—'

His telephone rang.

'Yes, sir. I understand,' he said after listening to the caller speak for what seemed, to Arora at least, an eternity in purgatory. Assuming that the Secretary—for who else would Almeida address with such deference—had conveyed a decision, Arora looked at the old man with expectation.

'Listen carefully. Any moment now, Justice Sinha of the Allahabad High Court will step into his courtroom to pronounce judgement against the Prime Minister. He will declare her election to Parliament null and void, and bar her from contesting elections for the next six years. Do not ask how we found out. I am afraid the authorisation we requested will be sacrificed at the altar of political self-preservation.' He sighed. 'Onward we move along the brink of vermilion boiling, pray we do not become the boiled uttering loud laments.'

It was the twelfth day of June in nineteen seventy-five.

CHAPTER THIRTEEN

The Hague (the Netherlands)

After a long wait, one that became more frustrating with each hour that crawled by, Malathi finally received instructions from Almeida on the tenth of July. The request had been denied, he told her, after due consideration had been given to the potential diplomatic fallout from a failed assassination attempt on foreign soil, or even a successful one. More than a fortnight after the PM and her advisers had assumed absolute power, it was their opinion that any action that might trigger a foreign affairs crisis was best avoided at a time when internal governance was in shambles. Almeida's message did not specify if the lady herself had agreed to place her own political survival above national interest, or if it was just her coterie shielding her from an impossible decision. Malathi no longer cared for the difference. As a mid-level consular officer in the embassy, she had seen the apparatus of the state swing into action as soon as a state of emergency had been declared, performing impossible contortions with practised ease to explain why it had been necessary for the government to place democracy in a coma to save it. An older man seated next to Malathi at an address by the ambassador had likened it to 'twisting themselves into Jalebis' and had later observed, rather loudly, that 'one doesn't establish a dictatorship to safeguard democracy'. Reaching back and paraphrasing Orwell to make sense of their circumstances was a double-plus-ungood, and he was recalled to New Delhi a few days later. Big Sister was apparently listening.

As for Option B, identifying a suitable person or team within the Dutch security establishment would be tricky. Counterintelligence agencies tended to make it more than a little difficult for foreign diplomats to get a glimpse of their inner workings, and in her case, a mere glimpse would not do. Had they tasked her with penetrating the BVD a year or two earlier, she might have had a reasonable chance of success. But the BVD had never been a target for the Wing, and with good reason: foreign agents that set out to penetrate the host nation's domestic intelligence agencies had, on an average, a substantially reduced life expectancy; successful recruitment happened, more often than not, before the recruit joined counterintelligence, not after. It needed oodles of time, a luxury Malathi could not afford because, as Almeida's message clearly said, surveillance had to continue till the case was handed over. She had already sent word to Mark to avoid taking unnecessary risks: no more midnight strolls, no more climbing garages to take a closer look. Despite the reduced profile, the transition would place the de Wits, Mark, and the doctor who acted as the go-between in danger of being discovered. She was worried that a convincing case could not be made without sharing photographic evidence, and that would make it trivially easy for the BVD to trace the house from which Khan had been placed under surveillance. From that, the elderly couple who had rented it would be a hop, skip, and jump away. Mark could flee to Berlin and lie low, but the de Wits would need more time and preparation to disappear effectively. Worrying about their safety kept Malathi awake at night. There was no scenario in which her network would survive the transition unscathed.

August brought with it news that worried the team at Main. The Resident at Brussels, in a cable to Almeida, mentioned that a diplomat from the Pakistan embassy there had been non-grata'd back to Islamabad. Sulfikar Ahmed Butt, Third Secretary and top thug in the Resident's estimation, had been caught by Dutch intelligence while trying to purchase a few thousand high-frequency inverters. The Dutch had protested to the Belgians, and the latter had obliged. The language used in the cable made it evident that the Resident had been tickled by

Butt's asinine efforts: it began and ended with a reference to Pakistan receiving a kick in the Butt. Almeida frowned at the cable, not amused by the witticism. He asked Arora to investigate further. In a cable to Malathi, Arora recounted the entire episode, asked her to corroborate the account, and requested clarification from Veerman as to whether or not those inverters were related to URENCO's centrifuges in any way. Having failed to find a suitable entry point into the BVD, Malathi was in the midst of trying to recruit a bureaucrat in the Ministry of the Interior when Arora's cable arrived. As it demanded a response "posthaste", she made another trip to Almelo.

Veerman wasn't particularly pleased to see her, but invited her in for a cup of coffee anyway; it was becoming a pattern. Moonrise was still missing, but there was a small heap of empty beer cans in the living room behind the sofa, mostly Amstel. In response to her casually worded query, Veerman replied that his anonymous complaint had resulted in no changes at all.

'Khan is still a part of the Brain Box, and gets to read and copy designs and planning documents,' he added. 'I thought for a long time of blowing it up—you know, writing everything down and handing it over to the boss, but…it's as if they don't care about their own secrets. If they want to put a dodgy Pakistani in the Box and ignore my warning, well, then, fuck them!'

His tone was flat, uninterested. Malathi thought she could smell beer on his breath. He continued staring at a blank wall as Malathi offered careful platitudes. A few minutes later, her cup nearly drained, she asked if he had ever heard of the company from whom Butt had tried to buy inverters. The name had an immediate effect. Veerman's gaze sharpened and rested squarely on Malathi's eyes. He blinked rapidly and nodded, but wouldn't speak. She did not need him to. Thanking him for his help and repeating her advice about staying anonymous, she got up to leave.

'Did he try to buy from them?' Veerman asked, suddenly.

'It wasn't Khan personally,' she replied.

'Please leave,' he said.

She closed the door behind her and left him sitting alone on the sofa, his head in his hands.

A dossier meant to be shared with a foreign intelligence agency couldn't be a simple dump of every relevant document and photograph; that would give them insight into each source and compromise entire networks. What foreign agency would pass up such an opportunity? The first question any half-competent operative would ask on reading a surveillance report of Khan's handler's routine visits would be about who had carried out the surveillance: without that information, the report would lack credibility. One of his first steps the BVD would take on seeing the surveillance photos would be to identify the vantage point from which they were taken, and the person who took them. Malathi needed to address this line of enquiry within the dossier without betraying her agents, a tightrope walk made worse by New Delhi's insistence on continuing surveillance till the last possible moment. The subtext was clear: the safety of her agents did not figure prominently in New Delhi's grand calculus. The task had been made even more challenging by the varying objective. When Mark had taken photos from the garage roof, his directive had been to zoom in on the documents. Those pictures showed specifications and blueprints or they showed Khan's windows and the backs of two male heads. Had New Delhi asked then, he could have waited longer and taken some that tied up the close details with a distant view identifying the two men. Without such intermediates, the close-up details weren't unimpeachable in their own right and would need corroboration. That, unfortunately, meant exposing Veerman to the designs of the BVD.

The more Malathi pondered, the clearer it became that she would have to throw the young man to the wolves. None of the photos and surveillance logs she had to offer would have the same impact as a transcript of his debriefing, but the inquisitors would demand the source's identity. She worried that someone broken by Mark and her over one night would become a vegetable when the BVD inquisitors were done with him. They would go hard at him; inquisitors always did, regardless of which agency they worked for, unless circumstances mitigated their intensity. It was imperative that they believe he had done everything any civilian in his position could reasonably be expected to do. An anonymous warning delivered over the phone wouldn't cut it—the manager could easily deny any recollection of it; anyone with a modicum of an instinct for self-preservation would. Veerman needed a firewall between himself and Abdul Khan, a warning delivered in writing in his own name. It would have to be timed carefully around her own dossier; too early and the investigation initiated in response would not benefit from the dossier; too late and anyone with half a brain would connect the two, putting Veerman's sincerity in doubt. To ensure he didn't crumble under pressure and reveal that she had asked him to complain, the suggestion had to come from someone else. He needed to believe that he had chosen to complain once more, not anonymously this time, despite Malathi's advice. It had to be the only truth he knew, something fundamental within him, something the inquisitors couldn't peel away.

She had gathered copies of every piece of hard evidence: surveillance reports from Amestelle, photos from Karachi airport, Veerman's debrief, pictures from Amestelle, and detailed biographies of every ISI officer with whom Khan had ever been photographed. To those she added the cable from Brussels, relayed by New Delhi, that tied Sulfikar Ahmed Butt and his attempted purchase of high-frequency inverters to Khan. It took nearly a fortnight, between keeping tabs on surveillance, maintaining her other networks, and pursuing the official at the Ministry of the Interior, to thoroughly redact each and every bit that could be used to identify the sources. She was sleeping in her office on most nights to save time, and washing in one of the embassy's bathrooms; even then, she only managed a couple of hours of uninterrupted sleep every other day. Satisfied that the evidence would not blow the covers of any of her agents, she began writing a narrative that provided chronological context, tying each piece of evidence into a tale of treachery that she hoped would be impossible to ignore: 'For at least eight months, a mole in the Brain Box at URENCO has been providing a foreign government with detailed plans and specifications for URENCO's G-2 type centrifuge. The foreign government seeks to use those plans to enrich Uranium for the purpose of developing nuclear weapons.'

It would become the most significant document ever written in the embassy at The Hague.

Sometime in August, she sent word to the de Wits to prepare for departure. They took a day to scrub each and every surface within the house, wiping away their fingerprints and removing any other evidence that they had ever been there. Mark began wearing surgical gloves around the clock, hoping to avoid the need to perform that tedious task again.

One night soon afterwards, while the rest of Amestelle was fast asleep, a taxi pulled up to the house. It departed three minutes later, an elderly man and woman seated in its rear, and headed for the airport. Johannes retrieved a handbag from a locker at Schiphol and walked with Hendrika to a hotel nearby. A room had already been reserved for them. After checking in, they opened the handbag. Hendrika counted twenty thousand guilders, thrice. The bag also contained two train tickets for the next day to Rotterdam Centraal and instructions for disappearing for a year. In the bathroom, they burned the documents they had used for renting the house and checking into the hotel, then flushed the ashes of Johannes and Hendrika de Wit. A little after 5 a.m., just before the shift at the hotel front desk changed, they checked out. The doorman saw them walk, hand in hand, towards the airport.

Veerman's sneer made it plain that Mark was no longer welcome at his apartment. Mark pleaded, making far too much noise for a late night visitor, and Veerman finally relented; he let him in, but pointedly refused to offer him a seat.

'You have to formally complain to your superiors! You must! When they catch Khan, they'll find out about you. The only way to protect yourself from—'

'I complained in June. They did nothing,' Veerman spat out.

'A phone call can be denied, you fool. You must write it down and submit it in person. Take a copy. Insist that whoever you're offering it to sign the copy in acknowledgement. That will be your proof. Otherwise, you'll be suspected of treason, and believe me, you don't want that to happen.'

The sneer had disappeared. Mark sensed that, deep inside, Veerman was flailing for options.

'If the security agencies don't believe you, they'll assume you helped Khan,' Mark said, every cell in his body exuding urgency. 'You'll get the death penalty. I can't stay any longer. Do it tomorrow. For God's sake, save yourself, Frits. Good luck.' Mark exited the apartment before the idea of using him as a witness in his defence could occur to Veerman.

Four hours later, he quietly slipped into the house at Amestelle.

'It's done,' he said.

'Did you act the part?' Malathi asked.

'Yes. I told him he should ignore your advice and make a formal complaint to save his own skin. He thinks I'm some renegade who tried to help.'

Malathi nodded. It had been her idea.

'Get ready. You may have to leave at a moment's notice,' she told him before leaving.

The dossier was almost finished. New Delhi would review it. Once it was green-lighted, Malathi would give Mark an hour's notice before setting events in motion. Till then he would stay to keep watch, with her relieving him for a few hours once every two days.

An hour after dispatching a copy of the one-hundred-and-thirty-seven-page dossier to New Delhi in a diplomatic pouch, Malathi took an unmarked car from the parking of a small apartment she had rented through a cutout and drove to Amestelle. It was early evening, three days since her last visit; finalising the document had occupied almost every moment of those seventy-two hours. After parking a few streets away, she made her way to the house and entered it just after 8 p.m. Mark looked ready to collapse, having been awake throughout the three days that she had spent holed up at the embassy. She took over surveillance from him, and he was snoring gratefully before all of him had even touched the mattress.

An hour later, Khan's handler drove up to seventy-one, stood outside for a full minute looking at houses up and down the street, then rang Khan's doorbell and entered. Malathi made a note of the anomalous behaviour in the surveillance log for the twenty-second of September, then returned her eyes to the binoculars. She wanted to ask Mark if he had ever noticed the handler so overtly display caution, but took pity on him when she saw how deeply asleep he was. Forty-five minutes later, Khan emerged from the house carrying a suitcase. He was followed by his handler, who helped him load it into his car's boot. Khan rushed back into the house, emerging with a handbag a few moments later. There was an edginess to their movements, which Malathi diagnosed as anxiety. After dumping the bag in the rear seat, the handler sat at the steering wheel and gestured for Khan to get in. They argued. Khan stormed back into the house, returning a minute later with Mrs Khan.

"Mark!" Malathi hissed, urgently. "Wake up! Something's happening!"

119

Khan was kissing his wife and hugging her tightly, unwilling to let go. The handler leant across the seat and said something. The couple ignored him. He shouted, and at last they broke off. Khan walked to the passenger seat like each step was an ordeal and seated himself next to the driver. By now Mark was awake and standing next to Malathi. She tried to explain what had happened. Mrs Khan was sobbing, her shoulders shaking violently. Her husband reached out and held her hand. The handler shouted again. Khan pulled his hand back and slammed the car door shut.

They had to be followed. Mark offered to do it, but, in his grogginess, he slurred his words.

'The handler will spot you in a minute,' she replied.

Mark's bio, which she had been sent from New Delhi long ago, mentioned that his skills did not include vehicle-based surveillance. 'Keep an eye on the house. I'll return as soon as I can,' she said.

She exited the house at a normal pace, but dashed to her car once the handler's car had sped past her and rounded the corner. It took her a few nerve-wracking minutes of driving and intuition to regain sight of it. She followed it into Amsterdam. She had been sure they were headed for the airport, but the handler drove past it without the slightest drop in speed. Following at a safe distance, she tailed them to Aalsmeer, then along Kudelstraat before they stopped at a payphone. The handler alighted and made a short call. Malathi watched from a hundred yards away. It was nearly 11 p.m. The handler looped back and drove towards Aalsmeer. Having driven at a steady speed for most of the way till then, he sped up on Kudelstraatweg. Exhausted from lack of sleep, Malathi struggled to keep up. Any moment now, she told herself, he'll turn into a lane and try to shake me. She suspected she had been spotted, but there was no backup to allow her to disengage for a while. He turned into Beethovenlaan, heading east. She followed through Jupiterstraat, then back northwards along Lunalaan. After looping around Gluckstraat, they headed back towards the west along Beethovenlaan.

Malathi was now certain, based on the evasive turns he was taking, that she had been spotted. He was trying to shake her off; they couldn't proceed with whatever had been planned as long as she stayed with them. Khan was fleeing; she knew it with certainty. The thought of calling the police crossed her mind, but, without knowledge of his destination, she had no way to ensure that he would be caught. Besides, he was in a car bearing diplomatic plates. The police couldn't touch him until he exited the car. Malathi had no choice: she had to keep up. All she really wanted to do was to curl up in bed and sleep. Well, she didn't even need a bed, she thought wryly. The car seat would do just fine. She could pull over to the shoulder and take a short nap. Something inside her snapped and she shook her sleep off. This was not the time. After the operation, she would request a desk job in New Delhi, preferably one that allowed regular hours and ample time to sleep. She cursed herself again, half-heartedly, for ever giving in to Arora's honeyed description of life in the shadows, then laughed it off. No, she wouldn't say no to his offer even if time turned back and she faced that decision once again. This life had had its fair share of rewards and she had no complaints; well, except for the lack of sleep. The handler indicated a right turn, the amber lamp on the tail flashing in earnest. But there was nothing to their right except a lake. Craning her neck to peer into the darkness for some sign of an unlit bridge going across it, she completely missed the truck that came from Haydenstraat to her left, its headlamps switched off.

The truck ploughed into her car, finally allowing her some sleep.

CHAPTER FOURTEEN

On an unusually sunny morning in October, Jagjit Arora stood outside the embassy at Buitenrustweg and, having given the security officer his visiting card, waited to be allowed inside. He looked up and down that picturesque, tree-lined street and marvelled at how diplomatic enclaves all over the world looked and smelled the same. The embassy at The Hague was smaller, but it brought back memories of Berlin. He was transported to Tiegartenstraße. Standing outside the brick-red building with his wife that evening, they had been waiting for a taxi. He couldn't remember the destination, just that it was a social event at some embassy or consulate. A junior staffer had called out his name, then run over with a cable. It was unencrypted. "Captain Vivek Arora has been reported dead in the Sialkot sector on 15 September 1965," the cable had said. Arora had crumpled the cable in his hand, hoping to hide the news from his wife until they were indoors and alone, but his wife had seen it in his eyes. He remembered how she had opened her mouth to scream, but no sound had emerged; her eyes had blamed him that day, though, and every day afterwards. It was the moment his whole life had unravelled.

Arora breathed deep to clear his head. The morning air at The Hague was crisp. He hadn't wanted to travel to Europe, but Sablok had taken news of Malathi's death badly. Arora had seen his hands shake, and the poor fellow had spent the next half an hour vomiting in the restroom. There was nobody else to travel and tie up loose ends, so Arora had to gird himself. Despite an adult life entirely spent straddling the grey line that circumscribes shadows, and seeing too many lives ended prematurely, he had not, as he had thought he would after '65, become immune to grief. Four days had passed since Malathi's death. The dossier had been reviewed. The security officer, having verified over the phone that Mr Verma was indeed welcome inside the building, opened the gate and escorted him to the grandest office within, his attitude now deferential: the cable from South Block had indeed reached the ambassador.

The top diplomat greeted him with solemn grace and offered his deepest condolences. Arora had enough grief to contend with, so, after the thanking the lanky thirty-three year veteran of the Foreign Service, he made a rather abrupt pivot and asked for the keys to Malathi's office and her safe.

'Nobody has been allowed into it since that night, I hope,' he added for good measure.

The ambassador assured him, while rummaging through his own safe for the keys, that she always kept her office locked, and nobody but the ambassador himself had had access to it.

'And I haven't been in there, of course,' he added.

Arora nodded, a vigorous but transient action that agreed that such a thought was unthinkable, of course, and that he, therefore, hadn't thought it.

Then, realising that the ambassador's attention was still on the contents of his own safe, Arora said, 'Of course, Excellency. That goes without saying.'

Having found the box of keys and removed the two that were needed, the ambassador shut his own safe and handed the keys over to Arora.

'Incidentally, Mr Verma, we have organised a condolence meeting later today. Would you care to speak a few words about her?'

'I'm afraid I'm not here to mourn her, sir. Her efforts must not be in vain; I intend to ensure that.'

The ambassador walked him to Malathi's office. Inside, he expressed sorrow once again and turned to leave.

'I do have a favour to ask, your Excellency,' Arora said. 'Would you be so kind as to arrange for me to meet the Minister of the Interior tomorrow? Any time would be fine.'

The ambassador stopped mid-stride and turned around.

'The Minister himself?' he asked, trying to hide his surprise. 'It would be most irregular…goes against protocol.'

Arora shook his head with deliberate impatience.

'Protocol doesn't matter anymore, sir. The operation Malathi was running is time critical, and it is imperative that I meet with the Minister. If my credentials as an Under Secretary are insufficient, please feel free to disclose my real employer—I'm sure you have figured that out. I am not Malathi's replacement, sir. It doesn't matter if my cover gets blown tomorrow. But that meeting must take place. There is a lot more at stake here than diplomatic protocol and we no longer have the luxury of gingerly conforming to it.'

'What is this all about?' the ambassador asked.

Arora said nothing. The pause stretched uncomfortably.

The diplomat blinked first. 'I'll see what can be done.'

Arora locked the door, then checked the burn bin: it was empty; she hadn't even left ash. Her desk was bare of any documents. On a smaller table in a corner stood the Teletext, half-dozen cables lying uncollected near it. He checked the sender details: each one was from his machine back at Main; he did not need to decode them to know that they were enquiries about the dossier, acknowledgement of the dossier, and finally questions about the Resident herself after she had not made contact for twenty-four hours. He turned his attention to the safe. The key slotted in and turned, but the safe also had a combination dial. Malathi would have changed the code often, but service regulations, put in place for just such a contingency, required all Residents to inform a particular section at Main by cable of their combination code. Before leaving for Amsterdam, Arora, with Almeida's permission, had obtained Malathi's most recent code. He prayed that she hadn't changed it again; breaking in would take up precious time. He dialled the combination: six times anticlockwise to the first number, three times clockwise to the next, once anticlockwise till the last number had lined up against the notch; the handle yielded and the door swung open. He found the black, leather-bound notebook under a polythene packet stuffed with currency, and looked for the most recent entries. Each Resident had his or her own system of recording particulars of their agents, as well as the procedure for contacting them: some wrote these in exquisite detail; others used pseudonyms, preferring to keep real names in their head. Malathi had used aliases, but luckily for Arora, he was certain that one of the last few written pages would be about Mark. It was a choice between two pseudonyms and Arora guessed correctly. He read the procedure carefully, dialled the phone number mentioned, and enquired about an appointment using very precise phraseology, making sure to use the fictitious name written under the heading "Exigent Circumstances". Ringing off, he returned to the ambassador's office and requested a car with diplomatic plates. Three hours later, he pulled over outside a cafe in Amsterdam and waited.

Mark tapped the passenger side window after fifteen minutes, give or take a few. Arora let him in.

'What's a museum exhibit like you doing here?' Mark asked, lapsing into his native German. They were meeting after nearly a decade.

'She is dead,' Arora replied. His words hung in the air within the confines of the car, funereal and ominous like a cold fog on a swamp at dawn. As Mark came to terms with the news, Arora began driving.

'Coffee?' he asked.

'No! That's all I've had for days. Coffee and biscuits, more coffee, then one more cup. Should we be driving in public like this?'

'It doesn't matter anymore,' Arora replied. 'What happened on Thursday?'

'Was that when…'

Arora nodded. 'They made it look like a car accident. What happened?'

Mark began narrating the events of that evening. When he got to the part where Khan rushed out with a suitcase and, after kissing his wife goodbye, set off with his handler, Arora shook his head over and over again.

'She should have seen through it,' he finally said, his voice heavy with sorrow. 'And why didn't you go in pursuit?'

He hadn't meant it as an accusation, but sentiments got the better of good sense. Mark gave him a silent, pointed look that registered even though Arora's eyes were on the road ahead. They drove on in silence. Apologetic about the insinuation, Arora softly asked him to continue.

'I stayed behind to watch the house. She told me to. We had been taking turns surveilling the house; she drove down for a few hours every other day so that I could catch some sleep. Nothing happened after Khan left that night. He returned before dawn the next day. Was that before, or after?'

'After.'

'He walked back to the house rather slowly as if debating whether he should continue or turn around and leave. How did they get her?'

'They lured her out,' Arora said through gritted teeth, tensing the muscles of his jaw to keep them from trembling. 'Took her on a chase across Amsterdam till it was late and the roads were lonely. A truck rammed into the side of her car, pushing it into a lake. The autopsy revealed water in the lungs. She drowned.'

Mark said very carefully, making sure his tone was just right, 'How can we be certain it wasn't an accident?'

'Because the truck had been reported stolen forty-eight hours earlier. Because after the impact, it did not stop but pushed the car nearly fifty yards, into that lake. Because the driver fled.'

'Ruhe in Frieden,' Mark said, crossing himself.

'I need you to bring the surveillance log and any photos and negatives still with you. Tell the others to leave right away.'

'The others left weeks ago; she told them to. Didn't want them caught in the BVD's net, she said. That's why she had to help me keep an eye on the Khans,' Mark replied.

Arora's face tightened even more, his knuckles white against the dark brown leather of the steering wheel.

'Scrub the house, then go to Berlin—take the first available flight. There's a bag underneath your seat; take it when you're getting down. Use the money in it for travel. Once you're in Berlin, burn your papers. Burn them, don't try to sell them on the black market. Hear me?'

Mark nodded. Arora drove to Halfweg-Zwanenburg, referring to a map of Amsterdam on occasion, and pulled over a mile from Amestelle.

'I'll wait for you here. Hurry!'

The ambassador pulled off a miracle of sorts, getting Arora a ten-minute slot on the Minister's calendar the next morning. At the

126

embassy an hour before the scheduled time, he invited Arora into his office.

'We meet the Minister in an hour, Mr Verma,' he said. 'Before we do, however, I need you to brief me about the agenda.'

Arora gave argument after vague argument, trying to convince him that he wasn't authorised to discuss the matter with the ambassador.

'And yet you're permitted to discuss it with a foreign public servant,' the ambassador replied, cagily. 'I understand the need for secrecy, and I would never go out of my way to gain information from a Resident. You, sir, are not a Resident. What's more, you're meeting a foreign official as a representative of our government. That puts you on my turf, and I refuse to help you until you brief me. If it assuages your conscience, I would be happy to call the Secretary (Research) right now and discuss this with him. If he doesn't authorise it, we can speak with the Foreign Secretary, then my minister, and so on. Regardless of what it takes, Mr Verma, I will have the information I need, or the meeting gets cancelled. One cannot cross the Styx without paying Charon his due.'

Arora had no instructions about briefing the ambassador; neither for nor against. He weighed the risk against his need to meet the minister and felt it was warranted.

'Excellency, this stays within the four walls of this room.' The ambassador nodded. Arora looked around and said, 'On second thought, let's continue this in her office.'

They walked to Malathi's office. Arora had greater confidence in her room being free of listening devices. Even so, he began speaking in a low voice. 'A year ago, my colleague and I tracked a team of senior Pakistani nuclear scientists to Amsterdam. They returned to Karachi after just two days. What seemed odd, apart from that, was that they were chaperoned by a mid-level ISI officer. Malathi did a lot of groundwork over months and finally led us to a metallurgist in Amsterdam, a man of Pakistani origin. He works for the ISI, stealing secrets from the Dutch nuclear establishment. Our experts believe his product will accelerate Pakistan's quest for nuclear parity with us. This,' he said, indicating the thick package he was carrying, 'was prepared by Malathi and sent to us just before she died. I intend to hand it over to the minister for action against the spy.'

The diplomat hung on every word. He lowered his voice, cleared his throat, and asked why they didn't just eliminate the fellow.

Arora let out a wistful smile.

'We wanted to, sir. Malathi had even come up with a clever way of doing it. But our masters worried about the fallout you would have had to contend with were something to go wrong. Ultimately, they decided not to risk turmoil in international relations—there's enough domestic chaos to keep them busy for years. That got Malathi killed.'

The ambassador nodded. Arora could see the disappointment in his bitter smile, but he was too seasoned a diplomat to verbalise it.

'I am truly sorry that it turned out the way it has. Had I been asked my opinion, well, we could have weathered it.'

The meeting with the minister never took place. Instead, they were met by a senior bureaucrat who wasn't very forthcoming about why the minister was suddenly busy that morning. Arora informed him of the spy and handed over the dossier. He accepted it with the grace of a petulant child receiving an unwanted gift, then offered homilies. The meeting ended four minutes early after the bureaucrat assured Arora that, should they feel it was warranted, the department would contact the ambassador. When the ambassador protested about the casual manner, the official calmly directed him to the ministry of foreign affairs.

Back in the car, the ambassador turned to Arora and said, 'Don't get your hopes up about action being taken.'

'I won't, sir. He was not surprised when we told him about the spy. He pretended to be, but his eyes showed boredom. I'll bet my pension they already knew, and have done so for a while. If they had any intentions of acting on our inputs, they would, at the very least, demand to debrief me about the contents of the entire dossier. One doesn't accept intelligence without corroboration, not unless one already has corroborative inputs from other sources. They know, Excellency, and they will not lift a finger to stop it. I can't believe she anticipated this so precisely.'

'What now?'

'Now I fly back to New Delhi. Would your driver be so kind as to drop me off at the railway station? I'll catch the next train to Schiphol.'

The ambassador insisted that he join him for a cup of tea at his office before leaving.

'We had that condolence meeting yesterday,' the diplomat said, handing a cup of steaming tea prepared in a very British manner. Arora masked his revulsion for the drink by pretending to be interested in the decor of the office.

'I'm sorry that I couldn't attend. I had to tie up loose ends,' he murmured in response.

The diplomat waved his half-apology away.

'Ever since she was posted here, there were some who whispered vile things. The late nights she spent at the office or outside, and her refusal to be the distressed damsel for her colleagues, was proof enough for some that her character was blemished. The fact that she was out alone in Amsterdam at midnight when she...They made the most of it. I've always wanted to tell the truth about her, about her remarkable character. She must have known they were spreading canards, gossiping about her as if she were some...Eventually one always hears what is said behind one's back. That's the worst part about all this for—'

'Don't blame yourself, Excellency. We see and hear much worse in this profession,' Arora said, his tone stoic.

'Of course. Forgive me, I'm getting old and sentimental.' A flush spread across the diplomat's cheeks as he said it.

Arora finished drinking tea in silence, then prepared to leave.

'Would it help,' the ambassador asked, 'if I applied leverage through Dutch Foreign Affairs?'

'Excellency, if you seek directions about this from South Block, they will advise against it,' Arora replied, carefully.

'If,' The ambassador said, looking Arora in the eye.

CHAPTER FIFTEEN

'He doesn't socialise,' the old timer had answered when Arora, then newly assigned to the Europe section, had asked about how approachable Almeida was. It was followed quickly, and softly, by a quip about how Almeida never ever appeared in photographs. Arora thought it was a reference to superior tradecraft, but the next statement about turning into a bat each evening and flying away put it in context. Another senior Case Officer alluded to Almeida in monastic terms and, a few months later, once Arora had been accepted by personnel in the section as one of their own, he heard the legend about Almeida's Jesuit origins. Each metaphor and tale had a hazy, third-hand quality to it; and yet each one seemed plausible. Even within a community of paranoid professionals, Almeida was reclusive to the point of misanthropy. Known to enjoy the occasional drink in the verdant watering hole so beloved of Delhi's babudom, he avoided conversation despite the packs of Administrative and Foreign Service types always on the prowl for gossip. When socials happened within the Bureau itself, around bottles of Teacher's and VAT 69, his peers and subordinates learnt to begin and end without him. Rumour had it that the Secretary himself was yet to be privileged by Almeida's company for a drink, and nobody he worked with had ever been invited to his

130

house. Even the longest serving of his section had only the vaguest idea about his residence being "somewhere in Civil Lines", the place where he stowed his coffin. Which was why one evening in December, when Almeida dropped by their office and invited Arora and Sablok home, Arora felt the need to ask, not once but twice, if he really meant it.

For Sablok, visiting the Chief's modest apartment, after having become a regular guest of sorts at Arora's, was a study in contrast. He found himself seated in a living room that was immaculate: the walls were bare; there were no photographs of family, no portraits of notable ancestors, and certainly no framed posters of halcyon meadows, mountains, and streams. A corner cabinet was adorned with a record player and a handful of records that he longed to examine, but wasn't on familiar enough terms with the old man to actually do so. The apartment also lacked the usual accoutrements he had noticed in other Catholic households. Arora, too, stood glancing around curiously.

'Wondering where I keep my coffin?' Almeida remarked with a laugh. 'I do not have one, of course,' he continued, turning to Sablok. 'Hanging upside down in the closet is so much more comfortable.'

Arora guffawed; Sablok smiled that half-formal, reserved smile that junior officers deploy when the CO's wife makes an observation she thinks is witty.

There were three empty crystal tumblers on the teapoy, next to a whisky decanter, crystal again, brimming with amber. The old man filled each glass and offered two to his guests.

'Single malt, eighteen years. To absent friends, gentlemen.'

Bringing the heavy tumbler up to his lips, Sablok tilted it just enough to let the hint of a sip in and savoured dry warmth all over his tongue. It was smoky and rich, reminding him for some reason of the smell of a tandoor before anything was cooked in it, but subtle enough that he had to really concentrate before a hint of citrus was reluctantly unveiled. Whole minutes passed without a word uttered, each man immersed in whisky and quiet reflection, until Sablok found himself tipping an empty tumbler and his awareness encapsulated the room once more. Almeida appeared to have drained his glass much earlier, leading Sablok to assume, rather incredulously, that he was quite used to drinking such beautiful stuff on a regular basis.

Noticing Sablok reach furtively for the very last drop, Almeida murmured: 'We have drunk Soma and attained the light that the gods discovered.' Then, after topping them up, he toasted the committed bureaucracy, 'To the eunuchs running the government.'

After they had all taken at least a sip, Almeida smiled serenely for a few moments.

'I am honoured to inform you, dear sirs,' he then said with a smirk, 'that Mr Abdul Qadeer Khan, middling metallurgist, part-time spy, and resident of seventy-one Amestelle, has fled the Netherlands and found safe haven in the salubrious climes of Karachi. He was accompanied on the perilous journey to Schiphol, and thence to his destination, by his wife and two daughters. The Dutch security apparatus, that uber-competent organ of the state, emphasis on organ, bravely did their level best to facilitate Khan's departure by standing around doing fuck all.'

Arora's nostrils flared and his hands shook. He did all he could to keep his voice steady. 'Just as she had predicted.'

Sablok set his glass on the table, the sickness in the pit of his stomach rising to mingle with memories of the last sip of whisky. He worried, among other things, that he may never again enjoy the drink.

'Indeed, just as she had predicted,' Almeida replied. 'But do not despair just yet sirs, for there is more. In response to my request, the leadership—and here I leave to your imagination the exact personalities involved in making these decisions nowadays because I am buggered if I know—has opined that while the death—their term, not mine—of our agent was "unfortunate"—theirs again—now is not an opportune time to indulge—and this part is verbatim—to indulge fantasies of revenge that may invite international opprobrium. Committed bureaucracy, as I said.'

Arora downed the remainder of his drink and slammed the glass onto the table, then recoiled at what he had done and inspected it for cracks.

'The leadership did not pay for that, Jugs; my inheritance did. Do try to be gentle.'

Ignoring his words, Arora delivered a stirring, bilingual exposition on the leadership and their female blood relations, their incestuous sexual habits, and the mechanism of their birth. Flecks of spittle took flight with the words, and some built up in the corners of his mouth. Sablok chimed in, the tendons in his neck straining to break free, with a considerably narrower, monolingual vocabulary that returned again and again, like a broken record, to the legitimacy of marriages in their families. Almeida continued sipping his drink.

'Now that you have purged yourselves so candidly,' he said after both his subordinates had relieved their suffering for the moment, 'allow me to give you a tiny bit of advice: when an inquisition is in office, and make no mistake there is one right now, such richly deserved sentiments are best kept to yourselves. I have already made myself inconvenient. Should word of your, ah, feelings reach them, I am afraid I will be sharing a cell with the hoi polloi.'

'We can't let this go, sir,' Sablok urged him.

'This is treason,' Arora muttered.

Almeida stood up and shut the windows.

'Use your bloody brains, Jugs. L'etat, c'est moi! Well, today she is the state, and the Queen cannot commit treason, can she? No, sirs; perish the thought.' His glass was empty. He filled it once again and sipped, dispensing with the toasts this time.

'We're surrendering to Jilani Khan!' Arora countered. 'If they get away with it, then as soon as they realise they can kill our Residents with impunity, things will escalate.'

The old man continued smiling into his drink as if enjoying a private joke or the memory of a lover.

'The Wing won't sit idly,' Arora blustered.

'And how on god's green earth will this massive entity find out?'

'From us,' Arora blurted. His face had turned a sinister crimson and the veins on his forehead appeared bloated, like pythons after a heavy meal.

'Congratulations! You have fallen afoul of the Official Secrets Act, Mr Jagjit Arora. Your prize is a long vacation in Tihar. On second thought, they may not need to invoke the OSA—they'll lock you up under MISA—much simpler that way—and throw away the key. Then where will your tandoori chicken and seekh kababs come from?'

'This is absurd, sir. If we let this go, if we do nothing in response, then there is no hope.' Sablok insisted.

'Over the course of this life, I have come to the conclusion—and

I suspect our friend here would agree—that clinging to hope ruins everything. There is no hope, Captain. There never was. Tantalus suffers because he wishes to eat a fruit or take a sip of water.'

'We must retaliate! Otherwise, it's all wasted,' Sablok exclaimed, worried that the conversation was digressing.

'Retaliation has not been authorised,' Almeida stated, matter-of-factly.

'Neither was our operation. Not initially.'

Almeida finally looked up from his drink and sized Sablok up. He was at least three large pegs in, but the eyes were clear and alert.

'I am an old man, Captain. I have seen more than my fair share of dawns and will be gone within a year anyway. Arora here is a walking-talking myocardial infarction-in-waiting, and besides, I do not think they make jail cells large enough,' Almeida said with a sharp laugh that caught them off guard. 'But you are a young man. There is much they can take from you, make you ache for it all till there is nothing else left of you but your longing. And when you have suffered even more, you will have great difficulty in believing in good fortune. Do not take trivially the power held over you by those who embody the law; their malice outlasts lifetimes.'

Sablok's thoughts circled back to his personal, never-ending winter of discontent. He had nothing to lose. He smiled.

'Very well,' said Almeida. Turning to Arora, he asked, 'Are you still fixated on treason?'

'No, sir. I'm with him.'

Almeida topped up their glasses once more, emptying the decanter in the process.

'Do not expect joy from the act, gentlemen. Heed Dumas: He who pours out vengeance runs the risk of tasting a bitter draught.'

At 7 p.m. on Christmas Eve, Mishra walked into Almeida's office with a single file. After a brief conversation about the weather, he signed the most recent document and handed the file over to the older man.

'Are you quite certain you need him for an entire year?' Mishra asked warily.

'I hope it does not inconvenience you terribly,' Almeida replied. 'It is amply clear to me that Captain Sablok has become rather integral to the operation; my Case Officer vouches for him.'

134

'No inconvenience, sir,' Mishra said, automatically, then added, 'but with Khan in Karachi…' He let the sentence hang.

'Have your people been able to track him down?'

'Not a sign of him,' Mishra replied, leaning back. 'Which leads me to believe the ISI are devoting a lot of resources towards screening him.' He offered a fake smile.

'It is nice to see you smile, Mr Mishra; a rare and encouraging sight. The way my Case Officer sees it, even with Khan advising them in person, they cannot make any headway without procuring almost all the components of his centrifuges. Considering the fact that all of Khan's experience lies within the European nuclear industry, they will have to go shopping in my neck of the woods; please forgive the clumsy metaphor. We intend to keep watch. I cannot imagine that they will be as cavalier as earlier, what with Butt being disgraced in August, but not for nothing can human wisdom be expressed as wait and hope.'

Mishra's smile waned.

'Sometimes, sir, when you release that genie of eloquence within, I find myself mourning that large swathe of my existence when I couldn't even read a single page,' he said.

'Someday that epoch and your actions in it will be written about and read with disbelief, Mishraji. Who knows, they may even make a movie, with Dilip Kumar playing you,' Almeida replied, drawing a hearty laugh from his peer.

'Care for a drink?' Almeida asked after Mishra's laugh died down.

'Thank you, but I have quite a bit to do before calling it a day.' Mishra rose from the chair. 'Captain Sablok is all yours. Whatever it is you're actually planning,' he said with a knowing grin, 'I wish you well.'

Arora had cabled Malathi's replacement shortly after drinks at Almeida's house and demanded a copy of Malathi's black book. It was an outlandish demand and the Resident refused. Arora wrote back, repeating his request in stronger terms, the shallowest veneer of courtesy cloaking utter disdain. Predictably, it kicked off a row that escalated all the way up to Almeida, each skirmish documented and archived for future inquisitors. Almeida sided with the Resident, leading Arora to respond with the grievance that without the contents of the book, an analysis of the circumstances surrounding Malathi's accidental death could not be completed. He asked, in the same breath, if the Resident would be so kind as to share the surveillance logs at the very least so that New Delhi may glean what little there was in them to glean. The logs weren't present in Malathi's office or residence, the Resident replied. Arora asked him to check again.

'And please be thorough this time,' he added.

The Resident sheepishly assured both Arora and Almeida that he would continue making efforts to trace the missing logs. The archived cables would paint, for any inquisitor who might be mandated to find apostates of the fledgling religion of Committed Bureaucracy that was spreading like wildfire through India's steel frame, a picture of disorganised bickering and bewilderment, and an utter lack of coordinated intent. Meanwhile, the logs referred to within them had arrived in New Delhi in October, having flown from Schiphol in Arora's coat pocket. They had been wrapped in yellow notepaper that contained verbatim copies of the relevant pages of Malathi's black book.

Sablok drafted a cable to the Resident in Paris, seeking all available information about Tahir Hussain, Third Secretary at the Pakistan Embassy on Rue Lord Byron. Arora insisted on sending it in his own name. The paper trail, he had decided, would lead back to him. The justification for the request had been easy to provide: Hussain's efforts throughout '75 as Khan's handler and the hypothesis that any procurement of components would likely go through him. The cable was honoured a few days later with a lengthy dossier on the Third Secretary that arrived through diplomatic pouch, its summary concluding unequivocally that Mr Hussain was, beyond the shadow of a doubt, the Pakistani Resident. Arora handed it over to Sablok in deference to the role he had played in Sylhet, devoting himself, instead, to a painstaking post-mortem of the surveillance at Amestelle. He suspected the Dutchman's second complaint, delivered after he was prodded by Mark, had led Khan's handlers to believe that they were being watched, but it seemed like a reach. Before proceeding, he needed to know.

A week after the Tahir Hussain dossier arrived, Arora petitioned Almeida to authorise surveillance on the Third Secretary at Paris, using the same rationale that had yielded the dossier. It was approved in the first week of January '76 with the rider that it be conducted at arm's length; the old man did not want any more Residents falling victim to their own sincerity.

1976, New Delhi (India)

At another round of drinks hosted by Almeida, Arora ventured the broad contours of the plan that was beginning to take shape. He proposed tapping into the Parisian underworld—the Milieu—for the last actor. Sablok protested that hiring local criminals meant involving the Resident, which would needlessly broaden the conspiracy.

'Besides,' he added, his eyes aglow, 'Hussain was in the car that Malathi was pursuing. He had to have an accomplice driving the truck.'

He and Arora bickered over the details.

'There is a third person here, someone who worked with Hussain but remained in the shadows. Even if we neutralise Hussain, this third person may carry on with the task of procurement,' Sablok argued.

Arora was resigning himself to Sablok's logic but had to play the devil's advocate. He knew what Sablok was angling for, and did not wish to see it become a reality.

'We're drifting from our objective here,' he said.

'Which is what, exactly?' Almeida intervened.

'Sending a message,' Arora replied.

'I thought we were seeking vengeance,' Sablok countered. 'All the more desirable if it retards Pakistan's march towards parity.'

'And would not the message convey all our sentiments, as well as a warning, if we unmasked the bastard who actually murdered her, and killed him?' Almeida remarked, effectively resolving the argument.

A record of piano sonatas was playing that day, and later, once the battle was fought and won, Sablok felt emboldened enough to peruse Almeida's collection. There was a sense of shared purpose among them, engendering an esprit de corps of sorts. Almeida was far more informal this time, but unfortunately, the familiarity also resulted in the eighteen- years-old single malt being replaced by plain old Teacher's.

CHAPTER SIXTEEN

Paris (France)

Thirty degrees Celsius in June was nothing compared to what he was used to, having lived through half a decade's worth of summers in New Delhi and a few in the Thar before that. But the humidity that hit him when he stepped out of the train at Gare du Nord soaked Sablok's clothes in sweat within moments. He blamed Arora for bullying him into taking a roundabout route to Paris instead of simply flying to Charles de Gaulle like a reasonable person, and cursed him for the discomfort of the past five days. The flight to Heathrow had been excruciating, with the aeroplane landing at Beirut, Rome, and bloody Paris on the way. The weather of the Isles built upon what the hours in the cramped confines of Economy had done to his leg and, by the time he reached Dover three days after landing in London, his left thigh was a throbbing wound. Lumbering across the cold and agitated grey waste, the ferry from Dover left him seasick; he disembarked at Boulogne-sur-Mer, his throat saturated with a vile mix of gastric juices and salty tang. Phrases uttered in an outrageous French accent somehow got him to Calais, from where the journey to Paris consumed the better part of a day. In all, travel from New Delhi to Paris took him five days during which he did sweet fuck all as ordered, all because the Case Officer was feeling particularly paranoid about de Gaulle's CCTV coverage.

'French permissiveness extends to sharing surveillance video, Captain,' Arora had argued. 'Leave alone a competent investigator on your trail for assaulting a Pakistani diplomat, even Jacques Clouseau himself would head to de Gaulle and go through arrivals from India to find the tall, lean South Asian seen fleeing from the scene of the crime. Flying to a neighbouring country and crossing into France as far away from Paris as possible will buy you time, something worth all the gold in Kubera's kingdom when the Direction de la Surveillance du Territoire have caught your scent.'

Those words returned to Sablok at Gare du Nord when a lovely French woman, dressed in a very Parisian peasant shirt and cotton skirt, sniffed the air as she walked a few yards alongside him, wrinkled her pointy, slightly upturned nose, and quickly walked away on heels that Sablok felt would have made excellent close-quarters weapons. He could feel the accumulated grime of the days since he had checked out of the hotel in London, and craved a bath hot enough to melt stone. The days of inaction were building up his anxiety as well. This was nothing like Sylhet: it lacked the physical demands of ingress through jungles and valleys, over mountains and across rivers and, instead, afforded all the opportunity his idle mind needed to indulge in self-flagellation. Unencumbered while he sat in the aeroplane, trains, taxis, airports, ferries, and hotels, it dipped into noxious memories and scribbled each one of his myriad failures in excruciating detail on the parchment of his thoughts. He hoped the bath would seep warmth into his leg and ease the distressingly sharp pain he now felt with each step; vitamin Scotch was quite out of the question during an operation. The leg would have to wait, though.

He limped towards platform three, looking for a sign that said "Consigne". On the morning he left London, he had received an envelope containing a key and a receipt for locker thirty-nine, both of which had travelled from Paris to London in a diplomatic pouch.

Inside the locker, he found a fat package roughly the shape and size of a manila envelope, only thicker. Muttering a quick prayer that the Resident or whoever had brought it to the locker from the embassy had been careful to avoid attention, Sablok secured it in his suitcase and hobbled out, forcing himself to remain calm. His leg was getting worse. Outside, he flagged down a taxi, stepped aside for another passenger to take it, then flagged another; this one took him halfway across Paris along an indirect route that looped around the Eiffel Tower, the Champs-Elysees, and the Arc de Triomphe a couple of times before dropping him off at a hotel in Montrouge. Inside his room, he examined the contents of the package: the backup passport with a valid French visa and entry stamp went into a drawer beside his bed, along with the keys to a car—a Citroen H van stolen a few days earlier from Marseilles—and a map of Paris showing that it was parked in the Nineteenth Arrondissement; the cardboard box inside the package contained four polypropylene syringes, a few needles, a device with a disk-like handle and a sturdy needle emerging from it, and two vials labelled A and B that contained clear liquids. He stowed the vials inside the bathroom cabinet, away from sunlight as he had been instructed, and the rest of the Frankensteinian paraphernalia inside his shaving kit. He had hoped for a handgun, but the package was now empty; he would have to manage without it. Swallowing two Ibuprofens, he ran a bath hot enough for Agni.

Already a narrow street, the carriageway on Rue Lord Byron was further constricted by vehicles parked on either side along, and sometimes partly on, footpaths. A continuous line of buildings rose from the inner edge of the walkway, which was only a few yards across; together with the parked vehicles, the buildings formed a walled channel of sorts that, in many places, obscured pedestrians from anyone not looking down at them directly.

Late one evening, Tahir Hussain walked back towards the embassy. The green Qaumi Parcham fluttered languidly less than a hundred yards away, illuminated by a halogen lamp. Hussain's mouth still salivated at the memory of the succulent Raan-e-Changezi he had just eaten, and the bottle of Cabernet that he had downed with it had left him a little tipsy, but in a happy, warm sort of way. He burped loudly, then rummaged through his pockets for an antacid. A moment later, the forty-two-year-old man with an expansive waistline fell to his knees clutching his abdomen as fire radiated through it, searing everything and leaving him unable to breathe. Some of the acidic wine came up as he retched, but he couldn't tell if he had expelled anything. His eyes had teared up, blurring the whole world. There was no noise except the loud ringing in his ears. The cobbles at his feet darkened. Was this what a heart attack felt like, he wondered with vague detachment. The doctor had warned him to cut back on red meat and alcohol.

Someone was reaching across his right shoulder to help him up. The Duty Officer at the embassy could rush him to the hospital. He would survive this.

Sablok wrapped his arm around Hussain's neck until his elbow lined up with the Pakistani's Adam's apple, locked the blood choke with the other arm, and pulled back with his shoulders, dragging Hussain with him into the van through its open side door. Hussain's mind fought through the trauma of a brutal kidney punch and realised that he was in trouble. Sablok's arm was squeezing his carotid arteries, cutting off the supply of fresh blood to his brain. They were inside the van now. Panicking, the Pakistani tried to reach for his left ankle, but bending proved agonising, and caused him to hesitate and wince. Tipped off, Sablok pulled back even more and hooked his legs around Hussain's waist, locking him in place. Hussain was covered in sweat, most of it his own, and gasping for breath. Less than eight seconds after Sablok's arm had locked into place around his considerable neck, Hussain felt lightheaded. His arms thrashed about in a final, desperate attempt at escape. Then, the world around him went black.

Sablok slapped a pair of steel handcuffs on Hussain's hands, binding them to each other behind his back, then locked his ankles into fetters. A thick steel chain and padlock held the two restraints together. Time was running out. Pulling the door closed, he took a pre-filled syringe from a box on the passenger seat and searched for a prominent vein on Hussain's forearm. Plunging the needle at a shallow angle, he drew the plunger back: there wasn't enough blood flowing into the syringe; he had missed the vein completely. Hussain coughed and retched; time had run out. Sablok rolled him over onto his back and stuffed a rag deep into his mouth, just as his eyes opened and his whole body convulsed. Tossing the syringe aside, Sablok grabbed the thick needle with a disk-shaped handle—a device called a Trocar—and sat heavily on Hussain's left thigh just above his knee. The Pakistani was now fully conscious, and struggling to free himself. When the restraints held firm, bewilderment gave way to fear.

Feeling below the immobilised left knee for an oblong projection on Hussain's shin bone, Sablok placed the needle of the Trocar on a flat area of the bone medial to the oblong and put his weight on the disk-shaped needle. As he twisted the handle back and forth, the needle pierced Hussain's skin quickly and the sickening sound of steel scraping on bone carried through both their skeletons. A few twists later, with an audible pop from the bone and a muffled scream from Hussain, the needle pierced the bone and cleared a path to the marrow inside. Hussain's body went rigid as thousands of furious pain receptors overwhelmed his brain. Sablok quickly withdrew the Trocar, leaving the needle in place, and attached the barrel of the syringe to it. He had to squeeze the plunger hard to overcome the pressure inside the marrow, but a few seconds later all the fluid had been injected. He could feel Hussain's body going slack almost immediately as the anaesthetic concoction, made up of Ketamine and some other drugs that Sablok couldn't be bothered to remember, reached Hussain's nervous system. Less than thirty seconds later, the hefty Pakistani was unconscious. Sablok confirmed it by elbowing him in the groin. No reaction. Sablok did it again; just to be sure, he told himself.

He listened carefully for any movement outside: footsteps, cries of alarm, police sirens. When he heard nothing of the sort, he patted Hussain down, recovering a small plastic bottle of antacid tablets, a wallet full of Francs, an unopened letter from Lahore and, strapped to the left ankle with a leather harness, a Beretta 950. Sablok drew the slide back part way to make sure a round wasn't chambered, then removed the magazine and checked the bullets; there were seven. Putting the magazine back in, he drew the slide back all the way to chamber a round, flicked the safety off and then on again, and kept the handgun in his right trouser pocket. Stepping outside, he casually surveyed the street; it was deserted. Nobody had seen him assault the diplomat. The embassy showed no signs of life either—its door and windows were shut, the green and white flag flaccid. His breathing slowly returned to normal and the pain in his left thigh, which had ceased to exist for a few adrenaline-soaked minutes, returned with a vengeance. Before driving away, he grabbed another syringe with anaesthetic, a smaller volume this time, and injected Hussain through the needle sticking half an inch out from his skin. Then he yanked the needle out; he wouldn't need it again. Wiping the sweat from his brow,

142

he laughed at the memory of how, in that morgue in New Delhi, he had failed so many times before finally placing such an intraosseous needle correctly into a corpse's shinbone. He was still smiling when the van passed the Pakistan embassy and had to stifle the euphoric urge to shout at the building. He would have to be content in the knowledge, he told himself, that he had abducted their Resident from right under their noses. It was sure to piss Islamabad off if they ever found out, and there would be some kind of fallout, but worrying about it wasn't his job.

An hour past Versailles, he turned left off the main road and followed a route he had scouted the previous day. Each turn led to smaller and lonelier roads until he was driving down a narrow path inside Rambouillet forest, which covered an area of nearly seventy thousand acres. At a particularly secluded spot, he drove off the mud path into the woods, turning sharply to avoid the ubiquitous oak trees. He killed the engine and lights once the van had crested a small rise and was out of sight of the road. It was pitch black, almost midnight. But for the sounds of the forest, mingled with the ticking of the cooling engine, all was quiet. Hussain was still knocked out, so Sablok stepped outside to empty his bladder. In the dark, he trod on an acorn, jarring the piece of metal in his thigh, and grunted. When he returned to the van, Hussain was moaning faintly. Closing the door behind him, Sablok pulled the rag from Hussain's mouth. In the light of a small pen torch, he saw Hussain staring back at him, the pupils tiny islands in a sea of grey.

'Good evening, Colonel,' he said. Hussain's eyes, blinded by the light shining directly on them, moved from side to side as he tried to locate Sablok's face. 'Your Beretta is in my hand, its barrel pointed at your heart, safety off, round chambered; it will remain that way for the duration of this…interview. We are deep inside a forest, at least thirty miles from the nearest human. And even if we are disturbed, my first action will be to shoot you, twice. Screaming is not a solution to your problem. Do you understand?'

By now, Hussain had located Sablok's face; he stared at him even though the dark interiors of the van meant that he couldn't make out any features. Sablok noticed that his eyes were alert.

'I understand,' Hussain replied, his voice faint and wavering. 'Who are you?'

143

'You don't know me, Colonel, so my name hardly matters. The sooner I have what I need, the sooner you can go home and forget I ever existed.' Sablok paused, then, enunciating each word slowly, added, 'And the sooner can young Afroz Khan, son of Colonel Ejaz Khan, return home too.'

At the mention of his son's name, Hussain lost what little composure he had been able to summon.

'You're bluffing,' he said, striving in vain to appear unruffled.

'We'll see,' Sablok replied, lapsing into silence. He let Hussain stew for a few long minutes, then continued, 'Ordinarily a resident of Lahore Cantonment, near the WAPDA office, young Afroz is visiting cousins who live near Karachi Grammar School. Well, he was. He spent mornings and evenings at Clifton beach and hoped to join the army like his illustrious father. Nothing wrong in hoping, I suppose. Tell me, Colonel, when did you last hear his voice?'

Hussain blanched. 'A week ago,' he finally answered, his voice losing defiance with every syllable.

Sablok laughed, relieved that the gambit had paid off. The unopened letter from Hussain's pocket had provided him with the material he needed to spin the story, and the Ketamine had left Hussain in a partial dream-like state, susceptible to suggestion.

'Well, I hope you'll remember it for as long as you live,' Sablok replied, his tone reflecting the smirk on his face.

Beads of sweat rolled down Hussain's jowls. Sablok decided to press his advantage.

'Shall we begin? You know what statistics say about abducted children who aren't rescued in the first forty-eight hours…It has already been a day.'

By first light, Sablok felt confident that he had all the information Hussain would ever part with. Initially, the Resident had betrayed no qualms when he was offered his son's life in exchange for the identity of his accomplice in Amsterdam, an immigrant shopkeeper who had been behind the wheel of the truck that killed Malathi. A chance remark about "that Mohajir" explained the lack of remorse. But as time passed and the Ketamine wore off, Hussain's willingness to answer questions began wearing off as well. Questions about Abdul Khan's location in Pakistan were met with denials. The captive Pakistani claimed he was just a small cog in an intricate machine, unaware of where the operator sat. Asked about the operation to procure centrifuge components, the details he gave meshed well with New Delhi's understanding, but there was nothing in them that could have helped the Wing disrupt the effort. The interrogation ebbed and flowed, but slowly Hussain began to get belligerent. Perhaps he had worked out that Sablok had bluffed about his son, or perhaps he had become emboldened by the possibility of their being discovered as the minutes ticked on. The fact that Sablok wasn't torturing him for information must have served to convince him that his captor wasn't serious, or that he lacked the brutality to pull off a true interrogation. Instead of replying, he began ranting about "weak Indians" and their lack of character.

'You send a woman to do a man's job, and hope to defeat the most accomplished and warlike men on the face of the earth?' he scoffed. Sablok did not say a word.

'Next time, at least send an attractive one,' Hussain taunted. 'Maybe then she won't be killed.'

Sablok wondered, as Hussain let out a hysterical laugh, how it would feel to castrate his captive with a pair of pliers from the van's toolkit before stuffing the organs into his fat, foul mouth. No, that would be too quick, he thought. Perhaps if he pulled his fingernails off, one at a time, then broke his fingers: grip one, bend it as far as it will go, then give it a yank until the joint snaps, wait for a few minutes for the agony to play out, then begin anew with the next one—ten fingers, ten opportunities. Then there were elbows: an arm lock would need the handcuffs to be taken off, but just rolling Hussain on his stomach and pulling on his wrist while stepping on his scapula would be enough to dislocate the joint. Rotating the arm backwards and upwards would tear the ligaments of the shoulder. Sablok had dislocated his own shoulder once, during training, and relished the idea of subjecting Hussain to that kind of pain. He could use the pliers to yank each tooth out of Hussain's mouth, then feed it to him. There were so many possibilities. As he shifted to reach the toolbox, he remembered Almeida's instructions and paused. Hussain did not deserve a clean death, but since Almeida had ordered one, Sablok would obey. Hussain was in the midst of a rambling, jingoistic outburst when Sablok made up his mind.

'Were you ever posted to Dhaka, Colonel?' That stopped the rant in its tracks. 'Of course you were. I remember hearing about you, the butcher of Dhaka University. One of ninety thousand prisoners of war, ninety thousand murderers and rapists. I know all about you, Ejaz Khan, even about your harem of Bangla girls—'

'I never did that, I swear on my son,' Hussain exclaimed, terrified of the sudden change in his captor's tone.

'But your colleagues did. And you sat by and watched them do it, didn't you? You call us weak. You're the stupid bastards that lost half your country in fourteen days. Fourteen days, Colonel. Those poor Jews in Warsaw held out longer than you did. And you call us weak! How I would love to take my time with you, Colonel, like I did with your patrols in Sylhet.' Sablok pushed Hussain back and sat heavily on his waist. 'But the rotten stench of your vile existence offends me.'

He grabbed the third syringe from the passenger seat, identifying it by the tape wrapped around its barrel.

'It is a shame that this forest doesn't have wild dogs or wolves,' he said, unsheathing the needle. Hussain stared at him through bulging, unblinking eyes. Sablok could hear his rasping breath. 'But I am told it has a lot of wild boars; they eat all sorts of meat, even rancid flesh such as yours.'

He plunged the needle into the side of Hussain's thigh and pressed the plunger hard. Hussain tried to roll his body and throw Sablok off, but the shackles afforded him no leverage. His breathing became even more laboured and his heart raced. His body seemed to expel every drop of water in it through the pores of his skin. A splitting headache bored through his skull.

'I'll let the Pathans keep your son,' Sablok whispered. 'You know what they say about Pathans and teenage boys.'

Hussain wailed. He wanted to plead, but his lungs were empty even though he had just inhaled deeply. The left side of his face had become numb. Why was the Raan-e-Changezi so heavy, he wondered. His wife would have more antacid. He had to wake her up. She would help him find their son. They had to rescue him. Why wouldn't she wake up?

'Your son will pay for all the sins committed by you and your colleagues in Dhaka, Colonel. More importantly, he will pay for the murder of our Resident at The Hague,' Sablok said.

Hussain's ears were buzzing loudly, but he heard each word clearly as if they were his own thoughts. He struggled to free himself. His mouth was full of saliva, but he couldn't swallow. It dribbled from the corner of his lips, down the fleshy chin. A hot knife burned through his chest. He gulped for air but inhaled his own spit. The blade burned hotter. The smell of shit overcame him. Why wasn't his wife opening the windows? Couldn't she understand that he needed air? Air…

After unshackling the corpse, Sablok pushed him out of the van. In the light of the pen torch, he could see red welts on the corpse's wrists from Hussain's futile struggle against the handcuffs. There was nothing Sablok could do about them now. The letter and wallet went back into Hussain's pockets. Sablok wiped his own fingerprints off the Beretta before strapping it back to Hussain's ankle. Then, taking care to avoid the soiled seat of Hussain's pants, he heaved the corpse onto his shoulder and walked, with considerable effort and discomfort, deeper into the forest. His leg screamed bloody murder and his lungs burned after a few yards, but he kept going. In the faint grey of an overcast dawn, he dropped him as far from the van as he could manage, the victim of a heart attack. The chubby face was contorted in a grotesque grimace, the physical manifestation, Sablok hoped, of the trauma of dying with the knowledge that his son would soon follow.

It began to rain as he walked back to the van. Sablok smiled, his mind already on Hussain's accomplice, the driver of the truck that had ploughed into Malathi's car. He would soon be dispatched. But even then, the question of Abdul Qadeer Khan and the secrets he had stolen remained unanswered. Hussain's interrogation had Sablok convinced that the answers were no longer in Europe.

The operation was about to pivot to Pakistan.

℘ The End ℘

ON HISTORICAL ACCURACY

Let Bhutto Eat Grass is fiction woven around a few strands of historical facts. These facts have been drawn from a variety of sources in the public domain. The novel does not claim, however, to be historically accurate even though attempts have been made to adhere, as faithfully as possible, to the time line of events that took place in India, Pakistan, and the Netherlands in the 1970s.

Let me unequivocally state that the chapters and scenes involving characters from the Prime Minister's Office and the senior bureaucracy are entirely fictional. In fact, with the exception of Abdul Qadeer Khan, every other character is fictitious. Any resemblance to persons living or dead is coincidental. Even in Khan's case, the motives ascribed to the character are entirely my creation.

The inner workings of clandestine organisations are based on other, richer works of fiction. Procedures have been simplified and organisational structures have been flattened in the interests of avoiding getting the narrative bogged down by mundane details.

A TIMELINE OF EVENTS

The events below are well documented. Among the plethora of newspaper and magazine articles, websites, and books on the topic, the author recommends *Deception: Pakistan, the United States and the Global Nuclear Weapons Conspiracy* by journalists Adrian Levy & Catherine Scott-Clark, which offers a wealth of documented facts about the origins of Pakistan's nuclear weapons programme.

—11 March 1965: Bhutto's famous quote about eating grass but developing nuclear weapons appears in the Manchester Guardian.

—7 December 1970: Sheikh Mujibur Rahman's Awami League wins 160 out of 300 seats in the National Assembly of Pakistan.

—25 March 1971: Pakistan launches Operation Searchlight to curb the Bengali nationalist movement in East Pakistan. It will leave between 300,000 and 3,000,000 civilians dead.

—3 December 1971: War breaks out between India and Pakistan.

—16 December 1971: With Lt Gen A. A. K. Niazi signing the

instrument of surrender in Dhaka, Bangladesh is liberated.

—20 December 1971: Bhutto becomes President of Pakistan.

—20 January 1972: At a meeting in Multan, Bhutto orders Pakistani scientists to develop nuclear weapons within three years.

—18 May 1974: India successfully tests its first nuclear weapon at Pokhran, Rajasthan.

—July 1974: Abdul Qadeer Khan writes to Bhutto offering technology to enrich Uranium for nuclear weapons.

—August 1974: Bhutto replies to Khan via a letter hand delivered by J. G. Kharas, Ambassador to Holland.

—December 1974: A. Q. Khan travels to Karachi with his family. He is escorted to Islamabad where he meets Bhutto. The PM urges Khan to return to URENCO and continue spying for Pakistan.

—August 1975: Sulfikar Ahmad Bhatt, an ISI agent operating under diplomatic cover, tries to purchase high-frequency inverters of the same specifications as those used in URENCO's G-2 prototype centrifuge. He is apprehended by Dutch Intelligence, who now begin to suspect A. Q. Khan.

—October 1975: URENCO shifts A. Q. Khan to a different section where he no longer has access to sensitive information.

—December 1975: Fearing arrest, Khan flees to Karachi with his family. He carries with him three suitcases filled with stolen blueprints and documents.

MOVING FORWARD

Dear reader,

The sequel, *Let Bhutto Eat Grass: Part Two*, sees the operation pivot to Pakistan. Sablok, Arora, and the Pakistan section of the Wing are in pursuit of Abdul Qadeer Khan, scrambling to stop him and Pakistan from building a Uranium enrichment facility before it can develop nuclear weapons.

If you have enjoyed reading this novel, please consider leaving a review on Amazon and Goodreads.

Thank you.

Shaunak Agarkhedkar

Made in the USA
Middletown, DE
06 November 2021